ALL RIGHTS RESERVED
No part of this book may be reproduced or transmitted in
any form or by any means, electronic or mechanical,
including photocopying, recording, or by any information storage
and retrieval system, without permission in writing
from the author except in the case of brief quotations
embodied in reviews.
Publisher's Note:
This is a work of fiction,
the work of the author's imagination.
Any resemblance to real persons or events is coincidental.

Copyright November 2020 – Ana Calin

Table of Contents

Copyright Page..1
CHAPTER I..4
CHAPTER II...38
CHAPTER III 57
CHAPTER IV 95
CHAPTER V..116
THE END..168

CHAPTER I

Achilles

Fucking great. Just wonderful. Now we have to babysit the demanding, the-world-belongs-at-my-feet aristocrat that is Melanthe Skye, the rich cripple's widow. She is Charles Skye's much younger wife, who sure as hell never gave a fuck about him, and whom I have been watching from a distance this whole month as a sort of incognito bodyguard. Never got close enough to even see her face right, but I know that I don't trust this cold woman.

Tonight, one month after the funeral, she's invited my brothers and me to her manor, as protectors of Darkwood Falls, to make an announcement.

"I decided to take Charles' place in the City Council," she says, facing the fireplace, her back to us.

Three of my brothers murmur, while Nero and I don't react at all. Princess sniffles into her handkerchief on the couch, Nero's hands on her fragile, black-clad shoulders. It doesn't look like she's gonna be over her father's death anytime soon, but apparently her mother already has ambitions far beyond his grave.

"He would have wanted me to have it," Melanthe continues. "With his seat empty in the Council, the others can do whatever they want with Darkwood Falls. They could steer it in directions you really don't want it to go either, Mr. Wolf." She glances at Nero, the alpha and her soon to be son-in-law.

She avoids showing us her face, even though it's just her daughter Princess and the five of us in the huge drawing room, her late husband's portrait filling the room with his presence from above the mantelpiece. The only reason I can think of why she avoids us is that she has some deep, dark and rotten secret. Like, for example, that she was the one who had her husband killed.

"Speaking of your husband, Lady Melanthe," Nero says. "We avoided the subject so far out of respect for your pain, but there are pressing matters that need to be discussed. We need to know what your husband shared with you about his relationship with the serpents. Any information could be useful. In fact, it could be gold."

"I told you before, Charles didn't make it a habit to inform me about his dealings. I know that he was financing the former mayor's campaigns, Sullivan's I mean, and I know that weasel of a man had something on Charles that kept him pumping money. But I didn't know Sullivan was a serpent until well, a month ago, when I discovered everything else..." She stops as if her pain chokes her, but her elegant back is straight as a rod, her shoulders not even a little slumped. It doesn't look like she's crying. It looks like she's faking it, holding the handkerchief at her mouth.

"I understand it must still be hard, believe me, I do," Nero's addresses Melanthe, his hands lovingly caressing Princess' shoulders, her red locks falling over his knuckles like silk over rocks. "And I understand you need more time until you're ready to talk about this, but Lady Melanthe, time is really of the essence here. There are so many open questions about your husband's death, extremely—" He stops, his mouth hardening as he wills himself to go about this with patience. "But, if it's easier for you, we can start with things unrelated to Charles' death. Such as how come you were granted so much freedom, visiting the world's greatest cities, when the other women of Darkwood Falls could barely go to the next town. While your husband—"

"Ex-husband," Melanthe corrects him brusquely.

Princess raises her head slowly, blinking through her tears as if she's just emerged from a lake of sorrow to reality.

"You mean *late* husband," Nero tries to clarify.

"Charles and I divorced four years ago," Melanthe says matter-of-factly, and finally turns around.

It takes my breath away for a few moments. This is the first time I've seen Melanthe Skye without a big black hat and an expensive widow's veil obscuring her face. This whole month, she's taken pains to hide, either secluded in this house, or tucked in the back seat of a black limo whenever she went to town with her chauffeur, Murray.

I cross my arms over my chest, my tattooed biceps bulging, my eyes narrowing. I keep a poker face, but the woman is impressive as fuck. It would take a blind man or a complete imbecile not to register that, and it would take a dead guy not to imagine her spread eagled for him at least for a few seconds. And all that even though she's the embodiment of the word 'lady', her skin like porcelain, yet the look on her face so stern one would be tempted to think she got it by bathing in the blood of virgins.

The expression 'highbrow' must have been invented for Melanthe Skye. She's got high-arched eyebrows, and a long, thin nose that's got class in itself. I wonder what it would take to see those green eyes turn from ice to a fire of primal emotions, or those lips to lose their tightness. She doesn't have her daughter's full mouth that expresses lust, her lips are considerably thinner, and tighter, but she's got the most sweetly shaped Cupid's bow. Lips that I can't imagine she's kept only for her much older, pruned husband to kiss all these years.

"We didn't want to upset you with the news, my love," she tells her daughter. "We were afraid of the effect it might have on you."

"Oh you mean like the ways it could have affected my development?" Princess reacts, speaking for the first time since we got here. "Mom, I'm twenty-eight! I was twenty-four when you got divorced, if what you're saying is true. You're gonna have to come up with a much better reason than that for not telling me, and you know what? Right now, even if you did, I probably wouldn't believe you."

"Lady Melanthe, with all due respect," Nero intervenes. "We're going to need the truth. The situation is dire for Darkwood Falls with the serpents lurking outside its borders, and the Council that could be eating at the town's core from the inside. Without your complete honesty we could be running this whole operation into the ground."

Her eyes sweep over all of us, and I think they rest on me just a moment longer than on the others.

"My daughter was, in any case, of central concern to both her father and me, Mr. Wolf, I assure you about that," she says. "But you're right, the Council was also an issue. Knowing that Charles and I were legally separated would have fucked things up pretty badly."

My cock stirs when that dirty word leaves her classy mouth, and I find myself wondering what other dirty things she might take between those classy lips.

"They would have gone after his power, his money, his estate, his business and, with me out of the way, they would have found the legal means to take over." She walks to the sofa, stepping next to Nero and touching Princess' hair. "The best way to protect his legacy was to keep our divorce a secret."

I lean my shoulder against the doorframe, arms crossed over my chest. The distance allows me to assess her moves, her body language, the inflections in her voice, and gauge whether she's telling the truth, without interacting with her at all. That's what my particular role is in this situation. I analyze her the entire time in the back of my mind, checking for any signs that she might be hiding something, or trying to manipulate us.

And I have a strong feeling that she is, indeed, keeping something dark and heavy from us. There's something bad behind those bright green eyes. Something suspicious even about her cold reserve, and her breathtaking beauty. The woman is supposedly forty-eight years of age, and yet she doesn't look a day over thirty-five. I'm not exaggerating. She's got perfect porcelain skin, and the red in her hair is softer than her daughter's, gentler on the eye. Completely natural, no gray strands, no dye. I imagine fisting my hand in it and tugging while banging that perfectly shaped ass, fucking this proud lady into submission.

"Yet with all due respect," Conan's deep, bass voice breaks through my deviant thoughts, thankfully keeping them from perverting to the point where it's not funny anymore. He's standing by the mantelpiece, his huge frame as large as the picture of Charles Skye presiding over the room. "That doesn't explain how you were allowed so much freedom. The women of Darkwood Falls have been kept from traveling for years. Your daughter found ways to sneak out of town, but you traveled out openly, completely free."

"I *am* a free woman." Melanthe juts out her chin. "I would have no man restrain me in any way, not even my husband, no matter his status or money."

"You're getting us wrong," I put in, finally stepping forward. Melanthe's eyes fly over to me, widening, even if only for a moment. "The women of Darkwood Falls are Fated Females, the only kind of women that werewolves can imprint on and become bonded mates with. The serpents have always known that, which is why they went to extreme lengths to make sure none of you made it outside the town borders, except under close observation. Fated

Females are a rare commodity, they always have been, you know that now. The serpents have been keeping this town under control for this very reason, to make sure we wolves never got to the women that we could actually mate with, and produce more of us. So what was special about you?"

Melanthe squares her shoulders, pushing her chest forward proudly. "All this started *after* I became based outside of Darkwood Falls. Besides." Her tight lips move slowly into a mocking half-smile. "You refer to Fated Females as commodities, things for wolves to imprint on for the purpose of procreating, and I'm not entirely comfortable with that. Maybe the serpents knew I would never play into the hands of a wolf shifter, and didn't bother with me. Besides, in case you haven't noticed, I'm well beyond the mating age."

"Wait a minute, just wait." Princess jumps off the XXL sofa with her hands up, fingers spayed as if she wants to start tearing at her own hair again. "Why didn't you tell me about the divorce, I mean what the fuck, Mom? You can't just avoid talking about the elephant in the room!"

Melanthe seems to soften a little. "It was a secret to everyone, not just you. We decided it was best that way. Besides." She takes her daughter's hands in hers. She's taller than Princess, and leaner, and more dame-like, but that ass, damn, it's the most decadent thing I've seen ever since we came to this town. The silk showcases it in ways I'm sure Melanthe didn't intend her buttoned-up, black dress to. "Your father wanted the two of us to be his only heiresses. With me out of the picture, the Councilmen would have found ways to get their hands on his legacy, and—"

"Really, legacy?" Princess cries, her neck swelling with rage, which at least seems to make the grief more bearable. "Or inheritance? Why don't you just admit it, you didn't want to lose the money."

Melanthe keeps trying to explain things to her daughter with calm, but more suspicion starts to bloom in my mind, too.

I look up at the picture of Charles Skye, who seems to be staring down at her with the bushy dark eyebrows of a man in his forties. A man in the prime of his life, a far cry from the shell of himself that he died as. A cripple in a wheel chair, his flesh withered on his bones. He must have been at least thirty years older than Melanthe.

I keep by the far wall, leaning against the doorframe, and watching the exchange between Melanthe and her daughter, and then Melanthe and Nero. Conan and Hercules, our two huge barbarian brothers that usually flank Nero in battle formation when things get nasty, decide to cut their visit short. They jerk their heads in the direction of the exit. The wolves we got guarding the manor outside need their headmen.

I nod and, as Conan and Hercules leave, Drago emerges from the shadows behind me.

"So what do you think," he inquires. He must have seen in my face that I'm starting to draw my conclusions.

"I think she did it. I know that Nero won't want to hear it, because he wants to spare Princess all the pain that would cause her, but the woman is hiding something."

"That something doesn't have to be murder. We've been investigating Charles Skye's death for a whole month now, and nothing points to her as the perpetrator. Besides, come on. You saw the body. It took a man, if not a beast, to do the old man like that."

"First of all, the man was a cripple, and he was very weak. Melanthe is young, and fitter than her lean frame makes it look. She could have taken her much too frail ex-husband. With him having left everything he owned to her and his daughter in equal shares, she also had incentive. She wanted to get her hands on the money sooner rather than later. Maybe she has a lover tucked away somewhere that she's tired of hiding." For some reason that sentence puts vitriol in my mouth, and judging by Princess' attitude and the volley of reproaches she's shooting at her mother, she's of the same mind.

"You're fucking someone aren't you?" she spews in her mother's face, her face distorted with pain as Nero holds her back. "Is it that blond beach boy of a chauffeur, Murray, or is it someone else who will leave you more manors and a bank in Switzerland?"

Melanthe just stands there and takes it, shoulders back, chin up, but her mouth is trembling. She's an elegant, cold statue but the signs of pain start to crack that perfect porcelain façade.

It's my job to read and interpret those signs, because I'm the best qualified to do it, especially when it comes to women. Drago may have some experience with the ladies, having been a callboy and all before he met Arianna, but I'm the one who seduced his way into rich women's beds and extracted information about their serpent ex-husbands and associates. I'm the one they sent into the bed of Clayton Ray's much younger wife, too, soon after Nero became mayor. Clayton Ray is one of our most vocal opponents in the Council, and Nero suspects he has the strongest ties with the serpents, whom he's aiding from the inside.

"Are you gonna do this the usual way?" Drago says in my ear as the conflict continues between mother and daughter. I keep my eyes focused on Melanthe, analyzing every little move of her body, every twitch of the muscles on her face.

"What do you mean?"

"You know what I mean."

"Of course not. Nero would fucking kill me."

"You know what, I actually think this is the one woman you'd never be able to seduce anyway."

"Not that you poked my ego, but." I cock an eyebrow at him. "What makes you say that?"

"Look at her. The woman is a block of ice. She doesn't have suppressed desires to appeal to. If you ask me, she's as much a cripple as her husband, only that on the inside."

"A good thing I'm not asking you."

"You know damn well you should. I used to fuck women for a living before Arianna."

"First of all, you didn't fuck them for a living, because we're filthy rich. You did it because you liked enslaving them, and having them pay for it, too. Second of all, ever since you imprinted on Arianna, you've been consumed entirely with her, especially since she gave you cubs. You don't a have a mind for these things anymore."

"Yeah, keep telling yourself that. I have fallen in love, but I haven't lost *all* of my touch." He bumps his fist against my shoulder, and steps inside the humongous drawing room.

"Ladies, please," he says, raising his voice. "Why fight about this now? Poor Charles would be tossing and turning in his grave to see you like this." He steps in front of Princess, and takes Melanthe's hands. His voice has dropped to a calming, pleasant frequency, but he's not even trying to be seductive, which puts me at ease for some reason. He tries to steer Melanthe towards the sofa to sit down, but she resists him like she's made of stone, so he remains standing.

"If you really want to do this, all right, fine." He looks over his shoulder to Nero. "We should let her get her former husband's seat in the Council. We need someone we can trust in their midst anyway."

But it's Melanthe that answers instead of Nero. "First of all, I don't need you to *let* me do anything. I wasn't asking for your permission, I was informing you of what I was about to do. Besides, as Mr. Nero Wolf as the mayor in office surely knows, my right to my husband's seat stands, because it's been written in both his will, and his contract with City Hall. Of course, those eleven bastards sitting in that council will try to strip me of those rights, and they would actually stand a chance if they knew about the divorce. Which is why I invited you here. I need your help to make sure that doesn't happen. Running for next term's mayor's office, Mr. Wolf?"

"I am," Nero responds curtly.

"Very well then." She looks from Nero to Drago and then to me, pondering something. "Nero, I had every intention to refer to you as Mr. Wolf all the way, but it's going to be difficult to differentiate between you and your brothers, so I will take you up on your offer, and address you by your first name. So here's my proposition. I will help in any way I can from my seat in the Council, if you make sure the councilmen can't get to my divorce papers that have been registered at City Hall—in secret, but still; they can be reached. Also, I'll have you know that, when this is over, I will not tolerate any kind of restrictions on my own freedom—or Princess'. She wants to marry you, fine, you have my blessing. You want to lock her up in an ivory tower under the pretense that you're protecting her, forget it. Alpha wolf or not, I will have you by the balls if you treat her like property or like a pet." She withdraws her hands slowly from Drago's hold as she speaks and then, with one long look at Princess who stares back full of reproach and anger, she turns on her heel.

She's facing me in full now. Our eyes lock, bright green on beastly yellow. It hits me that it could well have been the unusual color of my eyes that made hers stop on me when she first swept over all of us. The others are astonishing males, but my eyes always raised extra attention, because they channel the animal inside so starkly.

"Lady Melanthe," Nero calls. Melanthe just waits, not even blinking as she stares directly into my face.

"If you take your husband's seat in the Council, you must be aware it'll come with great responsibility and great danger," Nero says. "The Reaper, the serpents' leader, will come after you, as I'm sure he went after your husband."

"I don't need you to educate me in matters of—"

"You'll be in far greater danger than you've ever been all your life. And I don't even care whether you believe me or not, it's the way it is. The seat in the Council is gonna come with a permanent threat to your life, which is why I will have to assign you a protector. A bodyguard. A guardian angel. At least until the threat is disarmed."

"A guardian angel," she scoffs, giving in and looking back at him. "Rest assured, Nero, I have all the security I need. Murray, my chauffeur, can take over the task. Before he took up this job he worked as a security expect for quite a few VIPs in New York."

My jaw tightens. That Murray guy again. I'm starting to think that Princess might be on to something about her mother having an affair with the blond beach boy. But why am I even wondering? I'm not usually wrong about people, especially women. My brothers have been using me to study them from afar for a while now. I have experience, skill, and ease in using it, so why am I unsure about anything now? If I didn't know better, I'd say that I might have a blind spot for Melanthe. That I don't want to see the truth about her because it might hurt me in some way. Which, of course, is fucking preposterous, because I haven't felt that way about a woman since the one that initiated me in the art of pleasure.

"Mr. Murray is just a man. You need the protection of a shifter, Lady Melanthe, a werewolf," Nero argues.

"One of your brothers, I suppose," she quips.

"You must understand, those that would hurt you aren't normal men either."

"Murray is a professional. I'm sure he's more than capable—"

"Lady Melanthe, believe me," Nero interrupts. "It isn't discrimination when I say he simply cannot stand against a serpent shifter. It's like a cat fighting a Rottweiler. It might manage a few scratches but it doesn't really have a chance beyond that. To fight a Rottweiler with some chance of success, you have to use somebody its own size. Like a wolf."

It doesn't take more than one look at me past Melanthe to understand what he wants. Melanthe does, too, looking from him to me and back again.

"Oh you mean Mr. ..." She circles her hand in the air as if she tries to remember my name, but we both know we've never been properly introduced.

"Achilles—since you decided on first names to keep things simple," I say.

She measures me from head to toes like a queen assessing a slave before she decides whether to buy him or not. "So, Nero, you want to replace the beach boy with a muscle-bound, tattooed cover model?"

"I assure you, Lady Melanthe," I reply in Nero's place. "There's a story behind the muscles, the tattoos, and even all those magazines that I modeled for. A story that makes me perfectly capable of ensuring your safety, much better than the beach boy."

She arches an eyebrow, and hell. It's sexy as fuck. "Really? Because you don't look like a bodyguard. You look like a callboy." She glances at Drago to make a point.

"Appearances can be deceiving."

"Indeed, they may, but I doubt they are in your case."

"Why is that?"

Melanthe walks around me, her bright green eyes moving up and down my frame like scanners. "Your reputation precedes you, Achilles. You warm the beds of bored councilmen wives. I don't even want to imagine how many other mistresses sigh over you in other towns. You're a heart breaker. An opportunist."

That sends a blaze through my limbs, but I manage to keep my cool on the outside. She has no idea, but I guess it's typical of these rich broads to act like they know it all. If anyone ever was an opportunist, it was those who've sought to use *me*, not the other way around. But no chance the councilman's wife would have told Melanthe what happened, so how would she even know?

"You shouldn't believe everything you hear."

"You know as well as I do that those aren't just rumors, Achilles."

My jaw clenches. Sibyl Ray shouldn't have trusted anyone with this, not even her closest staff. I lock eyes with Nero, the look in his communicating the reproach—I should have taken more precautions.

"Is that why you have second thoughts about me protecting you, Lady Melanthe? You're worried I might seduce you?" I let the yellow in my irises flash as my inner wolf growls.

"Oh, I have no such fears, I assure you. But if you're going to be my protector, I will have you know that I won't tolerate you crossing the line, or even trying to. I would take such attention as an offense."

My pulse picks up, and I'm not sure whether it's the challenge, her pride, or seeing her face up close. One way or the other, Melanthe Skye is far from an ordinary woman. I take a step forward, closing the distance between us defiantly, but just as I open my mouth to reply I catch a strange trace of her scent. Something beyond the scent of her skin, beyond the scent of rose petals. It's something hormonal, something that comes from the very chemistry of her body.

An instant and a tiny twitch of her cheek later, and I know what it is.

I grin, holding her gaze. This ice queen has thought about fucking. So she is human after all. I do nothing to hide the twinkle in my eye.

"I assure you, I will be nothing but a proper knight for you. As for my muscles, you'll find there comes a time when they'll prove useful."

She stiffens and blinks as if she can't believe my audacity, her mouth tightening. "You have seduced many women in your life, Achilles Wolf, and you think you're irresistible, but believe me. I'm nothing like those women. I will never get myself tangled in the web you're so skilled at weaving."

"All right, but you'd be doing me a great favor if you dropped the attitude. It's not like you're a some kind of innocent flower."

"Excuse me?" she says through her teeth. I can see a blurred version of Nero folding his arms across his chest behind her, as if he were taking satisfaction from my reaction.

"You sound angry that I've been going around seducing women, but let's be honest here—there's no way in hell you've been out of Darkwood Falls for so long, with a young handsome chauffeur as your right hand and bodyguard, and remained faithful to your crippled, much older husband the whole time."

"You have no business making statements like that. You have no idea what my life has been like."

"You know what, you're right. It's none of my business. My only business is to protect you." I can feel the yellow in my irises intensify as I say these things. "No matter my reputation, or what you think I'm doing with other men's wives, I am one of the very few people that can keep you alive." What the fuck is this surge in my chest? Why do I feel the need to lean in to get at least a whiff of that scent I caught before?

"You need a bodyguard, Lady Melanthe," Nero puts in, his tone appeasing. "He's a very skilled security agent. He runs our intelligence as well."

"Intelligence? You mean he's a spy." Melanthe's words trail off as she realizes the implications. I grin. Yes, that's why I've been sleeping with the councilman's wife.

"You know what I've heard about men like you, Achilles?" she says. "I heard that you become emotional cripples in time. That you're used to getting women so easily, and that you have so many to choose from, that you can't actually feel anymore." She scoffs. "I guess when you can basically get any woman you set your eyes on, women become less valuable *commodities*."

With that she passes me by, heading towards the stairs.

"I will see you tomorrow, I suppose."

"Lady Melanthe, I've heard what you had to say, but I have a few things of my own that I'd like to set on the table before we do this."

She stops, one hand on the banister, and turns around, staring at me from the high ground. She keeps her attitude, but her cheeks are pink.

"Firs of all, I would like to fire your chauffeur. Fire Murray."

"Excuse me? No. What reason could you possibly have for such a request?"

It's Nero who answers in my place, showing that it's not just a whim. "Anyone we don't have profound knowledge about could be the serpents' man. They could have infiltrated him into your staff, they're very good at that."

"There's no way I'm firing Murray, and that's that," Melanthe decrees. "He's been working for me for years, has been accompanying me everywhere."

Rage starts a low burn in the pit of my stomach, and the muscles in my jaw begin to tick. This leaves no doubt. He's her lover. He's been fucking her, probably for years.

"You don't get it, do you, Mom," Princess intervenes, stalking over like living fury. I'm not sure whether this is some complex at work that a shrink would have a good name for, whether the grief for her father's death messed her up completely, or whether she's really got a good reason to treat her mother like this, but the girl goes ballistic. "Dad is dead, and the men who killed him could have manipulated that particular dick into your bed."

"Princess!" Melanthe reacts in outrage, but her daughter is on a roll.

"No, I've kept my mouth shut for far too long. For years you've found reasons to leave Darkwood Falls over and over again, shaking Dad and me off. You're used to getting your way, but not this time." She places a hand on my shoulder. "Achilles is your protector starting today, but he is also the one who calls the shots, is that clear?"

"Say what? I have never—"

"No, I know, you never. You're used to giving orders, not taking them, but now you'll have to live with it. Whoever killed Dad is still out there, and if you're taking Dad's place in the Council, I'll make sure you're not doing it for selfish reasons. I'll have you in *our* service, at *our* disposal, helping us save Darkwood Falls form the serpents, and helping us get our hands on the murderer. You cannot *afford* freedom anymore, Mom. You've had enough of it, and Dad and I had to pay the price. For all your money and connections—or, shall I say, Dad's money and connections—this time you'll have to play by somebody else's rules." She glances at me with a heartbreaking mix of pain and rage in her face. "Achilles is moving in at the manor."

"I am?"

"Like hell he is," Melanthe spits.

"It's the only way we can keep an eye on everything, and ensure your safety at all times," Nero says.

"That's, of course, if you didn't get Dad killed yourself in order to have your way freely with the chauffeur, and protection doesn't make much sense anyway," Princess spews, walking up the stairs to her mother like a stalking jungle animal.

A slap rips through the big dark vestibule. Even the portraits on the walls seem to change their expression to one of shock. Melanthe has just slapped her daughter, who now bounces back with a hand on her cheek, her eyes blazing into her mother's.

With one last, mortified look at me, Melanthe turns her back and runs up the stairs. The sound of her bedroom door shutting forcefully echoes through the manor, and I must say it makes me uncomfortable. There's something about witnessing a woman of such strength being humiliated that gets to someone like me.

And yet, what if Princess is right? What if the secret that I feel Melanthe Skye is hiding is related to her husband's death? What if she is, in truth, the murderer?

Melanthe

I SHUT THE DOOR BEHIND me, and rest with my back against it. My eyes closed, I fight to keep the tears behind my lids, but I fail. I collapse to the floor, burying my face in my palms and letting out a soundless scream that tears my heart apart.

She hates me. My sweet little girl with red curls that I used to tuck in with her little doll Lucretia now hates me, and I can't even blame it on Charles. Charles stayed here with her, looked after her, loved her and raised her while I felt that if I stayed in this house, I'd die a slow, painful death. I couldn't share my pain with any living soul, and I ran away, leaving her behind. I came back now and again, but it wasn't enough, not nearly enough.

And he let me go, creating for himself the image of a loving, forgiving husband that wouldn't even dream of denying his beloved wife anything. But in truth, he couldn't afford to stop me, not if he wanted to keep the secret that had bound us from the start buried deep in the recesses of both our memory. The secret that I've been carrying like a brick inside my chest for years upon years, a weight that I can't lose even now, with him dead.

I manage to get myself off the floor and head like an old wreck to the vanity, unknotting my chignon with trembling fingers, releasing my locks down my back. I lower myself onto the cushioned chair in front of the mirror, and stare at my face. The face of a distant stranger. When did I even start to feel this way about myself? Was it all those years ago, on that fated night with Charles? Or was it when the aging process started to reverse? For all I know, I could be some kind of Benjamin Button. Maybe my life goes backwards, and I'll end up a baby in a crib.

I straighten my back, and look harder at myself in the mirror. I can do this, I can finally take the reins and find out which councilman betrayed Charles and led to his murder. I reach behind myself to open the dress, thinking about my daughter, tears streaming down my face. She and I, we're broken forever. We'll never be what we used to again.

From now on, I'll be more alone than ever, exposed to memories that burn. At least I'm not the same room I used to share with Charles. I couldn't bear to stay in it, and not because of fond memories of him, but because of his presence. Somehow I can still feel him, lurking in the shadows in his wheelchair, the monster that only I knew was hiding just beneath his skin. And the presence is strongest in there, in the master bedroom.

I wonder if spy-guy Achilles Wolf has any idea what kind of a man my ex-husband really was. Bah. That young daredevil, what could he possibly know? Throw a pussy in his way, and his brains will descend into his dick in a flash. If he'd been there when it first happened, at night in a washroom under the stairs of a place I can't remember, he would have probably walked right passed it, too absorbed with his own inflated ego to notice that a little girl's soul was being mutilated.

"Melanthe?"

I snap around to see a figure behind the curtains swaying in the soft breeze.

"God, Murray," I whisper in relief. "I didn't realize the door to the balcony was open. Come on, close it before anyone sees you. How did you get in here without the wolves catching you?"

"They ordered me to take a break from the job, but didn't dislodge me. I still live in this house," he says, turning from my chauffeur into my dear friend within seconds—my very gay friend, but that's something the Wolf brothers will never know. Especially the smug male model. I'll never give him that satisfaction. Let him think Murray and I are fucking, see what's he going to do about it.

"How did it go?" He inquires as his arms lock around me. I hug him back. God, I needed this.

"It was hell," I say, trying hard not to choke on my tears. Murray lets go, crouching down by my chair.

I don't know why, but part of me wishes Achilles Wolf would walk in right now. Probably because that would make it clear that he doesn't have a chance to ever do with me what he did with other emotionally neglected women men are so eager to label as whores.

"Princess hates me." My throat hurts as I say the words. "Ever since that night when I found Charles, she's been deeply suspicious." I close my eyes tightly, trying to get a grip on the tears, but that only revives that night behind my eyelids. Charles in his wheel chair, his eyes and mouth open, the gaping wound in his neck. My eyes snap open as I suck in a deep breath. I'm glad I didn't show this weakness in front of the Wolf brothers.

"She doesn't say it, but deep down, she thinks I had something to do with it. She thinks I had him killed."

"But you didn't. And you'll prove it to her, soon. That's why you're taking his seat in the Council, to uncover who did this to him, and to show Princes that her father wasn't the angel she believed him to be."

"I'm not so sure about wanting to prove that to her, Murray. Her father was her idol. Before Nero Wolf happened, he was the love of her life. If the wolf hadn't imprinted on her, causing her to fall madly in love with him, I don't think she would have ever been able to truly love anyone else besides her father."

"But it's not fair that she keeps that image of him while trashing the image she's had of you. I mean, okay, I get it, you haven't been in her life as much as him, but she loved you. Looked up to you. She was happy whenever you came home, spent time with you. And the truth is you were always there when she was little, it's not like you were a bad mother." He tucks a strand of hair behind my ear.

"Just tell me what to do to give you comfort," he says when all I do is stare at the curtains swaying gently in the nightly breeze.

"Can you just... hold me tonight?"

"Of course." He stands and helps me up, his hands gentle as he takes me to the bed. He helps me out of the dress, too, unzipping it all the way down.

Achilles

RAGE BOILS IN MY VEINS. Look at her tucked in bed with her lover just above the head of her daughter

27

who is still crying her eyes out downstairs. Hadn't it been for Nero, she would have broken down completely after her father's violent death. As for Melanthe, it's now pretty fucking clear how much she suffers for having lost her husband. For all we know, she could have been fucking her chauffeur from the very start. Did she lie like this with him on the first night she found Charles Skye dead in the attic room? Was she glad that he was finally out of the picture?

I stay here perched on the banister, staring right through the swaying curtains at her bed. I can see the contour of the chauffeur's hands moving under the silken sheets, caressing her body. They're not fucking yet, but they will, no doubt, and I don't know if I have the nerve to stay here and watch without barging in there, gripping him by his throat and dragging him like a dog out of her bed.

But watching her is what I'm *supposed* to do, and protocol makes it clear I am only to act if she's in real danger. Until such danger presents itself, I am just to watch. But those plans were made when we still thought she would be sleeping alone.

As time passes, the rage in the pit of my stomach grows. Probably because I expect her to start kissing him anytime now. I imagine her stern lips smiling sweetly under the covers before they press themselves gently on his. Her white hands moving down the sides of his torso. I took a good look at the chauffeur, and while he's no wolf or shifter that would give him supernatural strength, he's a fine specimen. A young specimen that Melanthe must really be enjoying to the max after thirty years of being married to a much older man.

Every second I expect things to start between them, and it's keeping me on edge. I can see it happening before it does and yet, at the crack of dawn, still nothing has happened. Expectation dies down, and my muscles relax, but that doesn't mean anything. Most probably they have been together for so long they don't need to fuck that often anymore. Maybe Princess' pain actually had an effect on Melanthe, and she didn't find it in herself to pleasure her lover tonight.

I jump down from the balcony and make my way to the kitchen, where the cook is already working on breakfast. I grab some coffee, my hands a little too rough on the machine.

"Wow, someone's in a bad mood this morning," the cook says, his little eyes darting in my direction. He's a small round man in his fifties, and one of the few people I like in this town. "Had a bad night?"

"I suppose you can say that."

"Didn't get much sleep?"

"Didn't sleep at all." I lean against the counter with the coffee in my hand. "I'm your lady's new bodyguard. I watched—" Better not to get into the details. "The house. I watched the house all night."

"Night shift, eh? At least you get to take the day off."

I shake my head. "No days off for us wolves until the serpents' threat is dealt with." I pass him by and bump his shoulder. "Stay safe. Go straight home when you're done today. Try to keep out of restaurants and pubs for now."

"But you have to sleep sometime," he calls after me.

And he's right, but it's not gonna be now. First of all, I have to do some reckoning of the premises, the gardens, and the land belonging to the manor. We have a whole army of wolves securing the property borders and the town's borders, but I'm a control freak like that. The serpents have been creating way too many acolytes using those vipers they've been breeding and implanting into people. The others have discovered so many bearing the serpent tattoo on their wrists, it's become impossible to track them all down.

Now we've started scanning all those entering town, but the serpents stopped tattooing them, and while people aren't allowed to just enter and leave town just like that, the serpents' supporters helped 'import' them.

I step outside on the ground terrace with the coffee in my hand, scanning the gardens. They're fit for a countess' manor all right, the gardener working her scissors expertly along the decorative shrubs around the central fountain. Anyone could be infiltrated by the serpents, even her, the sturdy-looking, pumpkin-cheeked gardener. We have the town under control with the extra men we've got from Conan's excursion to Italy and those the Brigade of the Wolves sent, but the serpents break rules we'd never dare touch. Their success comes from inoculating people with vipers they grow especially for that purpose and infiltrating them into town using their supporters are only those we know about.

I hear Melanthe's voice behind me, somewhere in the manor, addressing her staff. Her meeting with the Council is set for eight o'clock, which gives her about an hour to prepare. I would do the same, but since we've only decided last night that I'd be accompanying her as her bodyguard, I didn't get the chance to set myself up in the manor. A matter best brought up as she's having breakfast alone at the long table in the dining room, all the doors open to let the daylight and fresh air in. I stop in the doorway and lean against the doorframe with the coffee in my hand.

"I see you're all ready to go," I tell her.

"You are not," she notes, spearing another piece of her scrambled eggs with her fork. She's wearing a long black dress today as well, one that hugs the elegant shape of her body, but doesn't reveal much of her skin. Her make-up is modest, and her hair is pinned up restrictively in a simple plait. The only jewelry she's wearing is the golden chain with the shell-shaped medallion that Princess said is the only thing that reminds Melanthe of her dead parents. I scoff under my breath. Last night fucking the chauffeur, today playing the unadorned nun.

"You left last night before we got to finish the conversation," I say coldly. "We didn't get to discuss my lodgings if I am to stay here and protect you at all times."

"You and your brother, Mr. Mayor, made it clear you don't need my approval for your decisions."

"No, but this is still your house, and us deciding who gets to live where is out of the question."

"Funny, you made decisions about everything else in my life." She pops a cherry into her mouth. I push myself off the doorframe and walk casually up to her, one hand in my pocket, the other one holding the mug of coffee.

"Not everything. If you'd asked us before you engaged in an escapade with your chauffeur last night, we would have strongly advised against it."

She chokes on the cherry, just like I expected. But, instead of feeling satisfaction, I leap over there, and pick her up quickly, knocking her chair back. I squeeze until she coughs out the tomato. But gratitude is the last thing she expresses, of course. She turns around in my arms and swats my chest, full force. I take a step back, but no more, as her rage blazes at me from her bright green eyes. The eyes of a cat that wants to scratch.

"You spied on me?"

"I watched over you. And you were supposed to know it was happening. We talked about it yesterday."

"We didn't talk about you violating my privacy!"

"You can't afford privacy under the circumstances, Lady Melanthe. There's much more that needs to be discussed, so whether you like it or not, you and I will have to spend some time with each other to set certain things straight. But let us start with one clear condition—whatever you tell me, let it be the truth. I can't protect you if you keep secrets."

"I won't tell you who I'm seeing and when."

"Then you're making my job impossible."

"I don't give a fuck!"

"For a lady, you sure like to take that word in your mouth a lot."

Her eyes are blazing as she's trying to come to terms with her rage. "How much of last night did you see?"

"I saw everything."

"Then you know that nothing happened between Murray and me."

Beyond the flush in her cheeks and the rage that pours from her, she sounds worried. Worried that what I discovered last night might cost her dear chauffeur his job. And deep down, I enjoy her covert fear. Let her worry that I'll throw that opportunistic bastard right out into the street for the serpents to have their way with. They probably infiltrated him into her life anyway.

"What I know for sure, Lady Melanthe, is that you spent the night half naked with a man in your bed."

"He had his clothes on!"

"I don't give a fuck about your kinks, or his. The only thing that interests me is to eliminate all danger from your immediate proximity. And, as much as you'll hate to hear it, Murray is a very big potential danger. He's your chauffeur, and obviously important to you, which means you have a soft spot for him, which makes him the perfect weapon to use against you."

She bites her lower lip, glaring at me like an angry cat. It sends heat to my dick, and I imagine for a moment this presumptuous lady kneeling down to suck me off. I manage to shake it off so that I can keep confronting her, but now that I have thought it, I know the fantasy will return.

"I won't let anybody push Murray out of my life. Not you, not even your brother the mayor."

Blood surges into my dick along with the fury that threatens to send the fur sprouting out of my skin. I step into her private sphere, staring down at her like I am her boss.

"How about your daughter, Princess? Might she have an influence over this?"

"Leave Princess out of it," she says through tight lips.

"I couldn't do that even if I wanted to. She lost her father in a very brutal way. The man who loved her and raised her, the man who was as much part of her as one of her limbs. The pain she goes through is so bad that not even her bonded mate, Nero, can pull her out of it. Not even when he joins forces with her two oldest friends, Arianna and Janine. And the only thing you care about is to keep your chauffeur in your life." I give her a once over to make her feel like everything she's not—small and insignificant. "Do you realize how pathetic you are, screwing your chauffeur?"

Her hand lashes up, striking me across my cheek. I see it in slow motion, of course. Us wolves have much quicker reflexes than humans, but I let her do it. I know damn well I was an asshole, and I deserve the slap, maybe I deserve a couple more. But the truth is I didn't even aim to offend. What I wanted was to provoke her to lash out. To shake her impressive control. If she's the one behind her husband's death, then this is how we're gonna get her to unravel. The question is, why do I feel the way I do about it, why the low burn of rage in my stomach? Why the pleasure at the thought of snapping the beach boy's neck? It's not like I'm normally quick to defend the dignity of a dead man who hasn't exactly been an angel either. There's something else at play here.

"Now that you've gotten the extra energy out of your system," I say calmly, "let us go over the essential stuff. I'm gonna stay in this manor as your protector, and for that I'm gonna need a room, where I can tend to some basic stuff. Unless you're ready to go with me to the Council meeting as I am now." I motion to myself. I'm still in yesterday's clothes, namely ripped jeans, army boots and a black tank top that shows all of my tattoos, definitely a far cry from what Melanthe would want to present to the Council as her bodyguard, namely someone in a neat suit. Someone like Murray, which is what she seems to like in bed, too.

Having spent so much time away from Darkwood Falls, being a beautiful young wife to a much older, crippled man whom she left for glamorous travels to the world's biggest and most vibrant cities, everybody knows she's been fucking other men. The chauffeur was at her disposal all the time, accompanying her everywhere, adjusting his style to suit her tastes. Spite rises in my throat. It would have been easier to bear if she'd been changing lovers, but having had the same one probably for years means that he's important to her on a deep level, and that makes me want to punch something. My wolf growls, wanting to rip throats open, particularly the chauffeur's.

"You can get the master bedroom for all I care," she says between tight lips. "It's luxurious, and you'll find all the amenities you can possibly desire, from a hot tub to your own personal massage therapist, at your disposal twenty-four seven."

"I don't need a hot tub or a message therapist, I need a room that's close to yours." There's tension in my jaw as I speak, my entire body now fighting to keep down the beast. The need to shift is overwhelming. It's the reaction I get whenever I sense enemies lurking around, but this time I know there's no enemy out there. It's like my body recognizes the chauffeur as a threat that needs to be eliminated promptly. "In fact, it would be best if you and I would share a room. That way I can protect you twenty-four seven." Fuck, did I just say that?

"Like hell we're sharing the same room."

"I'll have to ask you to stop the meetings with Mr. Vonn as well."

"You can't possibly—"

"I can, and I am. I am forbidding it." I won't tolerate that man close to her, not now, not ever. Part of me wishes he turned out a serpent acolyte, so I can kick him right out of Melanthe Skye's life.

"He's not a serpent acolyte. He's been in my service for many years now."

"And this town has been under serpent influence for decades. The old mayor, Sullivan, had been a serpent shifter forever, and no one got a hint until the whole thing blew up in their faces."

She maintains her cool, but I can see she can barely keep her chin from trembling.

"I can't have my life restricted this way."

"You know what, I can't believe you're putting up such a fight to maintain your secret night life. Your husband just died a violent death. Your daughter is so heart-broken, her soul mate fears she might never be whole again. With all due respect, Lady Melanthe, do you even have a heart?"

She lifts her hand to strike me again, but this time I catch her wrist in the air. She's so thin, and delicate, and yet everything about her emanates strength.

"You don't understand," she says through gritted teeth. "Murray and me... He's the only friend I ever had." It sounds like it's causing her pain to admit it, but I don't care. I don't believe her, not after what I saw last night.

"Tell you what. You don't have to feel alone ever again. On the contrary, I will move in with you, I'll be your room mate. Don't worry, I'll sleep on the floor," I add before she can protest. "And I'll keep my back to you most of the time, if that's what you want. But the decision is made, and this is how things are going to be. It's the only way I'll be able to effectively protect you anyway. Just make sure your lover doesn't get in my way, because if he does, there won't be a second warning. Now." I let go of her wrist, walking backwards and putting distance between us. "I'll go upstairs to *our* room, and freshen up. Have a coffee, or use the time to talk to your good *friend* Murray. Make the break-up as soft as you must, but make it quick."

CHAPTER II

Achilles

It's been weeks, and even though I managed to keep a cold façade towards Melanthe, I can't say it was easy. I didn't sleep on the floor in her room, like I'd professed I would, but took the room right next to hers, which can be easily accessed through a side door. I left it open most nights, with the exception of those when the chauffeur was away on business, which I made sure he was pretty much constantly.

But ever since, sadness settled in Melanthe's face as if it made a permanent home with her. It enrages me to the bone that the chauffeur is so important to her. The beast inside me roars, angrier than ever. If those two will ever get together again, it's gonna be over my dead body.

They'll probably meet again if things go Melanthe's way today. She and Nero have been working to get the support she needs from the people of Darkwood Falls, as well from other influential players from other towns. If she finally gets her seat in the Council today, Nero offered a whole team of security to remain at her disposal, so that I can go back to work with him and our brothers on more important things, like our future strategy. It hurts our operation to have someone with my skills stuck in a personal security job, when I could be helping in far more vital points.

So today, on what could be my last day as Melanthe's bodyguard, I thought I'd humor her and wear the kind of outfit she likes. She half-approved of my uniform that consists of slacks, and a perfectly ironed white shirt, but I just couldn't stand the jacket, so I left it.

"What do we got on the property borders," I ask in my headset as I step out of the house, my eyes sweeping over the garden.

"All good boss," the reply comes in the headphone. "As clean as yesterday."

And yet it feels different, the very air carries a strange scent. I narrow my eyes as I reach the car, leaning against it with my arms crossed over my chest, waiting for Melanthe. She'll be here soon, she doesn't like being late for the Council meetings, especially today, when the big decision will be made. The battle for the legacy of Charles Skye has been fierce and, as she expected, the councilmen are putting up one hell of a fight.

"Let's go," she commands, waiting for me to open the door to the back seat for her. Ever since I took over Murray's job, she's been treating me like a valet to make up for it. She's been trying to make me feel like shit the entire time, but that's not what bothers me.

What bothers me is that I haven't seen pussy ever since I started to babysit Melanthe Syke, and her proximity isn't exactly working in my favor. My eyes keep returning to her in the rear view mirror, even though I make sure she doesn't see that.

She keeps her eyes on her laptop, but I've learned to read the tightness in her delicate jaw by now. She's worried, and, knowing what she's thinking about, I get it.

There are twelve seats in that Council now, and before her ex-husband died, it was all men. They used to call themselves the twelve apostles, because they were leading Darkwood Falls to brighter days. Economically, Darkwood Falls is home to some of the most influential people in the States, among whom Clayton Ray. He owns ClayRock Mines—gold mines. He's one of the most important councilmen, and top of my list when it comes to who might have functioned as the serpents' rat. I used to sleep with his wife just before I got assigned the new job of protecting Melanthe Skye, in order to gather intel. He's also Melanthe's most vehement opponent, and he's a damn powerful one.

The moment we walk into the Council Hall, out of all of the councilmen sitting at a round table like Arthur's knights, Clayton Ray is the first man my eyes rest on. His antipathy towards Melanthe grows by the day, and he's not at all successful at hiding it. Sitting there, his back to the huge arched window that looks out to the impressive City Hall gardens, he resembles an angry piglet. He's small, and round, with rosy skin that looks dangerously delicious to my wolf. His small, darting eyes are framed by a V-shaped line across his forehead that indicates his people-hating nature.

I've done my homework on him, and fucking his wife was part of it. I found out he's got deeply seated psychological issues, and I've got ways to use them to our advantage when the time comes. Right now, I observe him watching Melanthe as she heads to her place at the table, which is right next to him. Her heels echo against the floor as she prances over like a queen. She puts on a great show, but I know she's feeling far from confident. With a man like Clayton Ray on her right, and Tanner Moreno, the media mogul, on her left, the air can get heavy.

Tanner Moreno is the complete opposite of Clayton. He's tall, dark and handsome, and so hairy you'd think he's a wolf too. He's unmarried, and no particular sweetheart out there that I could hook up with in order to discover his dirty little secrets. He runs a media trust that's host to a bunch of magazines for hustlers, which settles things regarding his regard for women. He dates a new model every other week, women whom he sure as fuck doesn't entrust with any worthwhile information, so I decided not to waste my time.

Melanthe takes her seat between him and Clayton, while I stand by the door, joining the others' bodyguards. They keep watching me from the corners of their eyes. I guess even after a few weeks they still haven't gotten used to the sight of me, and deep down I get it. I'm a wolf shifter, which makes me taller and larger than fully human men. Our bones are bigger, and our muscles, too, it's just how we're built. Even the leanest of us look larger than the average human athlete, simply because we're a mix of species. It's what makes my kind appealing to the ladies, too, and some of our advantages aren't exactly fair. But people don't know all the ugly stuff that hides under the shiny appearances. Beneath the steely muscles, the bright eyes and the chiseled jaws we're animals, beasts capable of such brutality it's not even funny. During our first century of life we can barely control it.

"So, the day has finally come," Clayton Ray says, glaring at everyone at the table from under his permanently frowning eyebrows. "This is the day when it's decided what's going to happen with Charles' seat in the Council—whether Melanthe Skye is keeping it, or whether she's leaving, and we get to elect someone from the town's high society."

The situation is tight for Melanthe. She and Nero have been working tirelessly to get all the support they could get, and I know she's eager to put this behind her. She looks like an unshakable headmistress in her seat, but I know the storm behind that apparent calm.

Councilmen's assistants hurry over with pads and phones, some of them with piles of papers. The documents gathered speak both in favor and against Melanthe, and I know she and Nero have put a lot of effort into making sure that her divorce papers form four years ago don't surface. The copies that were archived at City Hall are now tucked away in Nero's safe.

But, of course, that doesn't exclude the possibility that a particularly hateful councilman like Clayton got his hands on the court papers. All we can do is hope that he didn't think of the possibility that Melanthe might actually have no legal claim simply because she was no longer married to Charles at the time of his death.

Luckily, it doesn't look like he has something that powerful in his hands. His cheeks redden so much while he searches for something now, last minute, anything that could strike her down, that he seems about to combust. The hairs stand up on the back of my neck, and my wolf bares his fangs, ready to send the fur sprouting all over me.

I step forward, but Tanner Moreno reacts before me, holding Clayton back when he rises from his chair like he's ready to blurt all kinds of insults at Melanthe.

"Clayton, get a grip," he commands. Muttering dies down all around us. He's a commanding guy, and people tend to listen to him.

I stalk over to Melanthe's side, squaring my shoulders, making it clear I'm all the support she needs.

"I don't get you, Tanner," the piglet Clayton splutters in a rage. "Why do you even take her side? What has this woman ever done for you, or her husband, for that matter?"

He wouldn't dare confront Tanner under normal circumstances, but right now he's really beside himself, because the scales lean more to Melanthe's side than he expected. He tried really hard to move people to act against her, but Nero and I managed to block all of his attempts from the shadow. I close the distance between Melanthe and me, because it looks like he could actually lose his head and become violent.

As for Melanthe, she stays in her seat as if she doesn't give a damn about Clayton's hysteria. Not even a muscle moves on her face, but I can see the tightness in her hands as they grip the arms of her seat. I zero in on her hands. She's not wearing her wedding ring. I remember how numb she has seemed these past few weeks, strolling around her manor like a ghost. At night she'd wake up, go to the kitchen, make herself some hot milk, and stare out into the starlit night with her hands wrapped around the mug. She took many hot baths—something people do when they're starving for emotional intimacy. Her detachment and cold control right now are an illusion. Her depression is real. But her determination to find out which councilman is working with the serpents, and probably also had her ex-husband killed, override it. During these past weeks I've come to know these two things motivate her like a sacred fire.

"You will renounce your seat today, Melanthe," Clayton growls, slapping his piggy hands on the table, his eyes blazing hatred into hers. "You know damn well you're not suited for this position. You cannot fulfill your husband's duties, and fucking Tanner Moreno isn't gonna help with that."

"Clayton!" Tanner protests. "You're not only disrespecting Melanthe, you're disrespecting me as well. You have nothing to support that kind of claim." He sounds threatening, which takes the piglet aback. I'm focused on him, aware of every twitch of his pink flesh, of the adrenaline and the hatred running through his veins. He wouldn't get to touch Melanthe with a mere breath if he were to try, but I can't intervene before he actually makes a move.

I don't like Tanner Moreno, but his intervention does help things. The tension in my shoulders loosens, and Melanthe's grip on the chair arms relaxes, too, but Clayton still has venom to spew. His small eyes dart up to me, a glint lights up in them, and a moment later, Tanner is off the hook.

"I'm sorry, Tanner," he says. "I guess you're indeed not her type. She's done with the rich and powerful. She doesn't need them anymore. Now she holds the power herself, so she can fuck much younger men, like her bodyguard here."

Current runs down my spine, but it's not because of the intended insult. I'd normally rebuke something like this, but his words revive that movie in my head, that fantasy that was bound to return from the first time I thought of it. Melanthe and I, tangled together.

But Melanthe doesn't react half as well. She rises from her seat, her lips now a red line.

"Enough of these insults, Mr. Ray," she says, stressing every one of her words in such a way that no one dares even breathe while she speaks, not even Clayton. "I have let you work out your demons through me, but you, Sir, don't know when to stop. You're a bully. But you're not intimidating me. There are serpents out there." She points in the general direction of the window. "Serpents that want my daughter and me dead, or better yet, inoculated with vipers they would introduce into our bodies in ways I'm sure you'd take great delight to imagine. But not even they scare me, Clayton. I have seen things and been through shit that would make your posh ass wriggle more than it does when your little wife flogs you in the privacy of your red room."

Clayton gasps, and Tanner barely restrains a giggle. As for me, I'm fucking stricken—How does she know? She knew about me and Clayton's wife, now the secret sexual pleasures Clayton has her provide for him. This woman is full of dark surprises like Pandora's box, and I fucking love it.

My cock twitches in my slacks, and a strange emotion rises in my stomach. Something I've never felt before, because I've never met such a woman before, and fuck knows I've met many in my five hundred years.

Clayton steps back, trying to pull himself together, and probably to understand how come this kind of information has found its way into Melanthe's hands, but fuck me. This woman is resourceful, and she's not scared to play dirty. The look in her bright green eyes now as she stares at Clayton conveys a clear message—there's plenty more where that information came from, and she won't shy away from using it if he goes on attacking her.

"It is done, then," Moreno says, stepping between Melanthe and Clayton and addressing the rest of the councilmen at the table, their assistants and their bodyguards. "Melanthe Skye is our first councilwoman, and she's taking over for her late husband Charles. She has proven that she has influence, she knows business, and she's not afraid of the serpents. In fact, if we don't waste time plotting behind each other's backs, we might stand a good chance to beat those suckers once and for all, together."

The councilmen pause for a few moments, glance at each other, then nod in half-hearted approval. One of the assistants slips outside with the clipboard and an iPad pressed to her chest, going to announce the decision to the rest of City Hall. Nero is gonna be the first person she informs, while my attention returns to what's happening here, in this room. I step back into the background now that Melanthe is out of danger, but keep my eyes on her like a stalker.

Tanner doesn't leave her side, drawing closer and closer as she speaks with the other councilmen. Tanner is obviously happy with the result, but I discover that in one thing I agree with Clayton—he does want to fuck her.

Blood pumps through my temples, and my fingers curl as claws threaten to break through my skin. Not another asshole going after Melanthe Skye. I make my way over there, stepping casually between Tanner and Melanthe. He takes notice of me, measuring me up and down as if to assess his chances if things get nasty, then tries to get close to her again. I block his way.

"I'm sorry, Mr. Moreno. I'm like a warning sign. If you can see me, then you are too close. Mrs. Skye is under strict protection protocol until further notice from the mayor."

"You mean from your brother," he says, taking a provocative stance. "I may remind you my position is in no way inferior to his. And I have every interest in protecting a fellow councilwoman, too."

"I understand that, but it's against protocol. Anyone could be a threat. We even had to let her chauffeur go, and he'd been with her for years."

He sizes me up with a grin. He's got some balls, I gotta give him that. Most human men feel instinctively that they should back off. They don't dare provoke me any more than they'd dare provoke a lion, but this one seems to lack that common sense.

"Replaced by you, right?"

I stare at him with glowing yellow eyes, not even trying to hide the animal inside. Tanner takes a step back, but doesn't break eye contact. Something seems to be giving him a disproportionate sense of confidence.

"I suppose I can humor you today," he says. "You won't be working for Melanthe for much longer anyway. Now that she's secured her seat in the Council, you'll be relieved of your duties soon." He slaps my shoulder, hard enough to knock a man out of balance, but I don't even move. "So enjoy today. My team and I prepared a celebration for Melanthe at the pub tonight, since we were certain that she'd win. Treat yourself to a drink or two. It will most probably be your last night in her service."

He brushes against my shoulder as he heads back to the others, and it's all I can do not to grab him by his shirt and ram my fist into his face.

I hover around Melanthe, but keep my distance enough to give her the space to talk to people. Only when the doors open and she's invited to go outside and talk to the employees of City Hall does she lock eyes with me, and it's all I need to understand she still wants my protection.

I follow her outside, analyzing City Hall and creating her itinerary in my mind. It's information I'll have to make sure that my successors receive, and that they act on it exactly according to the protection system I create. Envy pools in my chest. I wish I could keep close to her, discover the mystery behind her innate sadness, the reason behind her nightly ghost-like strolls through her manor, even the story of her shell-shaped medallion she seems to care so much about.

But once the job of protecting her is torn from me, Tanner Moreno will be the first one whose life I'm going to take apart for information. Clayton Ray is already in the process of unraveling. All I need is another tryst with his wife.

The more people come between Melanthe and me in the City Hall, the more the reality of our impending separation becomes a sore place in my chest. Starting tomorrow, all I'm going to see of her is gonna be from a distance. She's going to rekindle things with Murray the chauffeur, or she's probably gonna start something with Tanner, who trails after her like a horny dog. He presents her to the people gathered in the main hall of the building like she's his to introduce to them, one hand on the small of her back.

I'm right behind them now, my nostrils flaring, and catching that scent that she sometimes emits. The smell of something perfectly intimate and womanly, her pheromones. I draw closer, wanting more of it. I tell myself it's only because it helps me assess how she's feeling, and therefore what she's thinking. People's chemistry says a lot about them, their scent communicates information, and in the case of Melanthe Skye, the woman with the façade of ice, it's particularly useful.

The scent grows stronger. She's either in distress, or Tanner's hand pressing on the small of her back awakens her neglected desires. A murderous rush flashes to my head, my skin heating up. A vicious need to crush his skull takes over me, and it's all I can do keep myself from acting on it.

He nudges her gently forward as the gathered people move to the sides to make room for her. The older women glare at her with anything but kindness, but the younger ones look up at her fondly. All except for her daughter Princess, whom I glimpse standing alone on the landing above the gathering, hands on the banister watching her mother as she's being led outside the City Hall.

I place my fingers at the headphone in my ear, requesting information, my eyes sweeping like a hawk's over the surroundings. I zero in on a few vehicles that seem suspicious, but it turns out it's all just VIP families of Darkwood Falls coming to congratulate Melanthe, and a few reporters from the local press. Nothing big, and nothing that will make it out of town. Everything seems secure in the end, but I can still sniff something on the air that wasn't there yesterday.

I stay behind just outside the threshold of City Hall as Tanner and a retinue of assistants and bodyguards are leading Melanthe away from me, down the stairs to the car. I need a few moments alone with the air, alone with the scent that floats on it. It's not serpent smell, at least not entirely. The trace of it started out faint this morning, but now it's more pronounced. I start after Melanthe, and by the time Tanner closes her door and makes for the driver's seat, I'm already slipping into it.

"Sorry, pal." I tip my fingers to my forehead in a mock-salute. "Today, I'm still her bodyguard."

I press the button, the window rolling up in his face as I drive away.

"I asked my brothers to secure the pub, and if that upsets Tanner Moreno, I don't give a fuck. He should have talked to us before he organized a surprise celebration. There's no way you're setting a foot in there until we've done a sweep." I lock eyes with Melanthe in the rear view mirror. I expect her to glare defiantly back at me, but she only looks exhausted.

"Suit yourself. I need to get home first anyway. I need a bit of rest. Besides, it's not even elegant to arrive first at your own surprise party."

At the next junction, I take the road towards the forest, and therefore towards the manor.

"I could kick Tanner for doing this." It's the first time Melanthe offers information She must be so tired she doesn't care who she's talking to anymore. "A party at the pub was the last thing I need."

I keep looking at her in the mirror as she rests her head against her seat, staring out the window. I watch her a little too long, until aggressive honking snaps me out of it.

"Fuck," Melanthe shrieks, grappling around herself for something to hold on to.

"Everything's fine," I reassure her as I bring the car back under control, my hands tightening around the wheel, my leather gloves squeaking. That moment of vulnerability as she rested her head back, exposing her long white neck with the bluish veins under perfect porcelain skin... that kind of vulnerability from a woman that's larger than life was bewitching.

She has a hard time breathing, gulping in air, her hands clawing like a cat's into the leather seat. I pull over with a screech of tires, leap out of the car and pull her door open so hard it's a miracle I don't yank it from its hinges. I help her out, and she does something I never thought possible—she leans her entire weight into my arms.

"Breathe," I tell her gently as I lean her against the car. The air is helpfully crisp. It's only afternoon, but clouds gather quickly in the sky, darkening it as if the night were rapidly approaching. We're at the edge of the forest, on our way from the City Hall to her manor. I wouldn't have normally stopped here, not with the scent of danger that I've smelled on the air all day, but Melanthe can't handle a confined place right away, I can see that.

She stares up at the sky, gulping in air, her hand folding into mine and squeezing. She wants me to stay, which makes me think that maybe it's safe to do more. I draw closer and press her into my side, trying to give her a sense of safety. Her breathing evens out slowly.

It's quite an experience, feeling Melanthe Skye so soft in my arms. Nothing hints at the fact that, now that she's recovering, she desires distance. She wants to keep close, despite her antipathy towards me.

"Incredible," she breaks the silence, eyes up at the clouds swirling slowly in the sky. "You're one of the people I like least, but you're the only one I feel safe with."

"I'm sure it's just a glitch."

She loses a small laugh, but chokes on it and grabs on tightly to my leg.

"God, your body is hard," she says, clearing her throat. I nestle her safely against my body.

"I think you just had an anxiety attack. It doesn't look like it was the first one either," I say gently, aware I'm treading on thin ice.

She keeps breathing rhythmically, in a way that makes me think she's practiced it before, avoiding my eyes and keeping hers up. It obviously helps her relax, and the more tension she loses, the more trustingly she leans against me.

I've held beautiful women in my arms before, but with Melanthe, the experience is unique. This is a woman that I genuinely believe could rule the world, and experiencing her fragility is intoxicating. I get a glimpse of her loneliness, of her very deep sadness, and the more I see, the deeper I want to dive.

"What you, your brothers and even my daughter thought was freedom," she says, as if she can't help but open up, "was in fact anything but. What I really wanted was to be here, with her. With Princess. Do her hair on her first date, wait up for her on prom night wringing my hands, talk to her about her first kiss. About her first night with a boy. I missed so much of my own daughter's life because... because I just couldn't bear to be here."

"You couldn't bear it? Why?"

She opens her mouth to tell me, but then she changes her mind. Her walls start to close again. A strange sort of despair rises up in the pit of my stomach. She started to open up, and now she's closing down again, what did I do to cause that? I grab her shoulders, and turn her to me. Her eyes fill with alarm, as if someone just slapped her out of a dream.

"What happened here that you felt the need to leave and stay gone?" The chauffeur comes to mind, and my hands tighten on her to the point that she grimaces in pain. "It was him, wasn't it? Murray? Or others before him. You loved other men."

"Let go of me, you brute," she commands, pressing her palms against my chest to push me away, but I can't let go. On the contrary, I pull her closer, locking my arms around her so that she can't escape. She's like a flower in the arms of a beast, so small compared to me, so easily breakable, and that does new and scary things to me.

"Why did you go, Melanthe? What kept you away from Darkwood Falls?"

"It's what he did to me!" she screams, and pushes herself off of me with so much force that I have to let her go. Not because she managed to shove me, but because her wish to put distance between us is so strong it would be a serious violation to keep her.

She breathes with her nostrils flaring like an angry animal, and as I get a grip again I realize I just fucking shot myself in the foot. She was this close to giving me the truth, and I blew it. My anger descends from my head, but it now finds its way straight down into my cock. Damn it. If I keep watching that porcelain face with the eyes blazing with the fiery resentment of a hurt animal, the emotion such a contrast with her physical frailty, all bets will be off. I step back and yank the door open, motioning towards the back seat of the car.

"Please." I manage to sound like I've regained my cool, but fuck knows it's a struggle.

She stands there in her black dress, her hands trembling, glaring like she wants to launch herself at me with claws out, ready to scratch and take revenge for how I made her feel. And I'm wiling to take it. I'm already fantasizing about her coming at me, beating my chest with her bony little fists, accusing me of being a heartless brute. But a breeze drifts through the trees, stirring the leaves and bringing over the scent from before, and snaps me out of the fantasy before it can go dangerously far.

I breathe in the scent, my eyes turning to slits in a split second.

"Melanthe, get in the car," I tell her, my eyes scanning the forest edge. She hesitates at first, but when I hiss, "Do it, now," she understands this is serious.

She slides quickly into the back of the car, and I slip into the driver's seat. I drive off, but crack the window, just two fingers, to keep my nose on the scent.

"What is it?" Melanthe asks in panic, grabbing the back of my seat, looking ahead between the two front seats.

"I'm not sure yet." I'd have to follow the trail, but that means leaving her in a safe place and, right now, there's no such place without me in it. "But we're gonna need to follow the trail if we want to find out." I glance at her, her face so close to me we're almost cheek to cheek. We're so close that the scent of her pheromones that's been driving me crazy replaces the scent on the air.

"I should take you to safety first," I tell her. "But the safest place for you is with me."

She turns her head, and our eyes lock. Like the first time, it's bright green on animal yellow and, like the first time, there's a connection there. Only that now it goes deeper, as if an invisible barrier has just been broken, and I'm being pulled at light speed down a rabbit hole. I know damn well what this rabbit hole is. Something terrible and irreversible is happening, right now, and there's no undoing it.

CHAPTER III

Melanthe

What was that? The prickle of energy that traveled from my chest to my scalp? It happened in a split second, but the aftermath is like endless waves washing over me.

I drop back in my seat, putting distance between Achilles and me. My jaw slackens, and I feel like I've just been smacked over my head. I'm aware of the speed with which the car is moving, of the forest flashing by me, but I'm not afraid anymore. I'm not even alarmed. I don't care about the danger lurking in the forest anymore. These waves of feeling are like a drug.

I look at Achilles' big hands in leather gloves on the steering wheel, the leather squeaking as he tightens them. Did he feel that energy between us, too? Every thought in my head starts spinning around him, as if the world—my world—is becoming all about this irresistible male specimen, and I don't have the slightest bit of control over it. I can't help exploring the feeling.

The sensation I had the first time I saw him comes back to me, as vividly as if it were happening now. Of all his brothers, he was the only one that drew my attention *that way*. I thought it was his animalistic yellow eyes that made him stand out like that, those eyes that spoke of murderous instincts, of a man capable of protection and destruction at the same time. Or maybe, as much as I hate to admit, it was those mean tattooed muscles that didn't belong in secluded Darkwood Falls, but on the cover of some New York magazine—which, as I found out later, was where he usually made a show of them. Or maybe it was the intense expression on that chiseled face that was so perfect it seemed like it had filters applied to it, or the playful twinkle and occasional smirk that reminded me of the power Achilles Wolf had over women.

And I made no exception. I only hid it better than others, and not even for the reasons you'd expect. Yes, he did have an effect on me, young and powerful as he was, like an irresistible animal. Of course, he is actually older than me, but I still felt like a cougar, which is something I'd never tolerate in myself.

But now that fantasy has broken through the barrier of common sense, and everything the world and society has ever taught me, of everything that I've come to expect of myself.

I keep looking at the rearview mirror, waiting for him to lock eyes with me again, so I can assess how *he* might be feeling, but he doesn't do it. He keeps his wolfish yellow eyes on the dirt road until the manor's gates appear in the distance. He pulls into the driveway, opens my door to help me out, and still nothing in his attitude is different. He blocks anything personal between the two of us, and I'm afraid to push, but he follows me up the stairs.

"I'm going to need to take a bath," I tell him once inside my room, where it becomes apparent he doesn't have any intention of leaving me by myself. "A little privacy would be welcome."

"We can't afford privacy now," he grunts as he checks behind the curtains. He moves the wardrobe aside, which requires inhuman strength, doing things he never has before. I open my mouth and close it several times, blinking, forgetting what I wanted to ask as he moves around the room searching for threats. He's focused and undeterred like a police dog on a mission, the white shirt almost bursting at the seams on his taut body. He's a big guy, but I think he's bigger now. Could it be that he's close to shifting? I've never seen him shift before, but I'm pretty sure something is different about him now.

"You mind telling me what exactly we're looking for?"

"I don't know, it's just this—" He creases his nose with a low, rumbling growl in his chest. "This smell I can't shake. It's been on the air since this morning. It was faint but now..." He looks at me, a short break in his focus, then he turns around. "You can change, I won't look. But I'll have to stand guard at the bathroom door. We can't risk you being alone for one moment. Whatever this thing is, it's close, too close."

I would normally argue with him, say no, but I've never seen him in this mode before. I can tell he's barely keeping the beast inside, which scares me, but excites me at the same time.

Now that he's checked the walk-in closet, I go in and start undressing, while he checks the bathroom.

"Was today the first time you caught that scent?" I call. "Or did you catch it before?"

He takes a few moments before he answers. "It was there before, but not constantly. Now and again, and it was really faint, fainter than this morning."

My skin crawls as I think about the possibility of actually having serpents closing in on the manor. One of my weaknesses, almost a phobia, that I have never told anyone about involves the movies I watched as a child with snakes slithering into houses, and imagining them crawling through the pipes.

"Does the scent—" I take a deep breath, and brace myself for the answer before I ask the question. "Is it the smell of serpents?"

Again that silence as Achilles thinks about it, and it's torturous.

"I don't know what to say," he eventually answers, his voice like the touch of velvet on my skin. "It's close to the smell of a serpent, but it's not only that."

I cross my arms over my now naked breasts, my nipples hardening. I close my eyes and sigh. Good heavens, how long has it been since I've felt the brush of arousal? It's feather light, but his voice and his presence are enough to do it to me.

"It's like serpent combined with human somehow, but not the same way they combine inside their acolytes. It's as if they're two different people, not the same body, and yet united. Melanthe?"

I'm reveling in the sensations in my body, sensations that I haven't experienced in a very long time. I didn't even realize that my hands have started moving down my body, slowly, goose-bumps rising all over me.

"Everything all right?"

I jolt from my reverie the second before his face appears in front of me, but it's too late. I'm standing stark naked in front of Achilles Wolf, and I think he knows I was touching myself while listening to his voice.

"Jesus," I yelp, snatching a folded towel from the nearest shelf, which is the first thing I can grab to cover myself. The realization of what just happened floods my mind, and heat blasts into my cheeks with mortification. The only lady-like thing left of me is my chignon. God, I haven't felt this ridiculous in all my life.

But Achilles keeps staring at me, not showing any intention of moving away.

"I'm so sorry," I babble, even though I'm not sure which one of us should be apologizing. I hurry past him, bumping into his arm as I do. I run into the bathroom and shut the door, turning on the water, the sound of it filling the room. I breathe out and slide down on the tiled floor by the bathtub, holding the towel over my chest and trying to get a grip on my breathing. I close my eyes, trying mental yoga to cast the sight of Achilles Wolf from my head as he stood in the doorway to my walk-in closet, staring at my naked body.

"Jesus Christ," I breathe through my teeth, squeezing my eyes tighter and running both my hands through my chignon to free my hair. I'm so mortified I just can't get over it. How will I ever look into his eyes again? I keep raking my hands through my locks, massaging my head harder, using the pain to distract myself from the embarrassment.

But when I raise my head I see him in the mirror, standing in the doorway behind the tub. I press my lips together, fury balling behind my eyes. This time, he came in here looking for it, and I can't be blamed anymore. I get up to my feet and turn around to face him, holding the towel over my chest.

"Achilles, what the hell?"

I stare daggers at him, trying to intimidate him, but it doesn't work. I don't think it's ever worked, but at least my sour attitude made him back off, maybe lose interest. Not this time. This time, he just stares at me as if it's his birthright, as if I belong to him in some way.

My tactics have failed for the first time since I can remember. Damn it, when did I lose my bully touch? I don't seem to have any hectoring effect on Achilles, but maybe that's because there's something shimmering right under his skin, like a threat he keeps under very tight control that costs him hellish effort. A second later, I see it. It's the beast in him that stares at me out of those bright yellow eyes. It's not Achilles, the man, the human being, the unbearably cocky male model that served as my bodyguard. It's the wild part of him, the one that will listen to no master but its own impulsive desires.

He walks inside, and I can't bring myself to protest again. I take my hand to my mouth, afraid that he'll read the forbidden excitement in my face. How long has it been since I had this leaping feeling in my stomach?

I back away, which isn't something I have done often in my life. In fact, the last time I backed away from something was on that doomed night with Charles, and I'm paying the consequences for that to this day. I fear that the consequences of whatever Achilles Wolf has in mind will be just as serious.

My back hits the cold tiled wall. There's nowhere I can go anymore. I'm trapped, watching my bodyguard close in on me. God, he smells so good. The cologne always smells fresh on him, that fresh sports scent mixed with man. If I stood a chance until a moment ago, now I'm doomed. If he touches me, I'll give in.

Water splashes over the edges of the buried-in tub, my head snapping in its direction.

"Achilles—"

He bends to the side and turns off the water before I can actually say what the problem is, as if he has eyes behind his back. He keeps eye contact the whole time, and the moment he's done he leans with his hands against the wall, trapping me between his arms.

"Achilles." I Jesus, I'm out of breath. My heart pounds so hard I'm barely able to form words. What can I possibly tell him? I will myself to go on. It can't be that this beast takes over me like this. "Please, I can't breathe. This is completely and utterly inappropriate."

"You're right. It is. Completely and utterly inappropriate." His face comes closer with every word. I can't see straight anymore, which prompts me to push my head back, but there's nowhere I can go. I'm blocked between the wall and this large man who is leaning in to kiss me.

My heart leaps into my throat the moment our lips touch, and I can't believe it's actually happening. It's hard to feel and hear anything but my raging pulse, my palms pushing against the wall behind me because I simply don't know what to do with myself. My mind goes completely blank. This kiss, it's anchoring me into my body like nothing has in longer than I can remember. Maybe nothing ever has.

All I know is that my scalp is prickling, my blood is racing, and the wolf's lips are closing over mine. His touch is long and sweet, as if he's living out every second of it as intensely as I am. He peels his lips off of mine softly, slowly, and when they disengage completely I find myself leaning in after him, but I stop in time.

"I've wanted this more than I realized," he says, resting his forehead against mine. His eyes are closed, as he's taking in the sensation of what just happened. As for me, I still can't believe it.

"I—" What can I possibly say? How should I even react? I should be stern, I should reject him, but instead I find myself raising my hands and placing them gently on the sides of his neck.

I sigh, closing my eyes, taking in the excitement in my stomach.

"What is this thing I'm feeling, Achilles?" I whisper. "I've never felt like this before. Ever."

His skin is hot, and I can feel the blood pulsing through his jugular. But he doesn't answer, he just stares at me as if he couldn't look away if he wanted to.

"Tell me," I breathe. "I know you understand what's happening between us, I can see it in your eyes."

"If I tell you, you'll never forgive me."

He leans in and kisses me again, and I can't bring myself to stop him. I just let it happen, my eyes open as his lips mold to mine. This time I kiss him back, wanting more of him. He pushes his body against mine, only his linen shirt between his rock-hard muscles and my naked breasts.

He moans into my mouth and parts my lips open, his tongue sliding in, his hand cupping my breast with the eagerness of a school boy touching a woman for the first time. I can't believe I'm doing this. I don't even recognize myself. I'm a mature woman taking advantage of the lust of a younger man. If I let this go all the way, I won't be able to look at myself in the mirror tomorrow.

I struggle against him, but he traps me between his body and the wall. He kisses me deeper, as if the wants more of me the more he gets. But there's something more to this, much more. There was attraction between us from the start, and yet I was able to deny it. Now, it's coming back with a vengeance, and I'm powerless against it.

My slit creams, and I start to squirm vehemently. I have to free myself from his arms before he realizes that I'm creaming for him. If he discovers the effect he has on me, I'll be mortified to death. But he pushes one muscular thigh between my legs, taking my wrists in his hands and pinning my hands to my sides against the wall.

"You want this, I can feel you do," he growls, his voice laden with desire. He surely already has a hard-on and the thought alone sends a jolt of current all through me. I lick my lips, unable to control my reactions, and blood shoots hot into my cheeks.

"I can't, Achilles," I manage. "We shouldn't. It's just... not natural, it's not okay." I refer to the age gap between us, even though it's not technically like that. At his five hundred years of age he's the older one, but in the eyes of the world I'd still be a rich wanton having her way with a younger man.

Achilles' eyes slip down my body, catching the glint of unbridled lust as they stop on my hardened nipples, then moving down the line of my abdomen to the light triangle of hair that masks my folds.

"Oh, Lord." I squirm, trying to get away from him again, but he pushes his knee up between my legs, keeping me in place. "Just let me go, I don't want to be naked in front of you." I beg with my eyes closed, my face burning.

"Why not?"

"What do you mean why not? It's completely inappropriate, outrageous," I exclaim.

"Shhh." He kisses me lightly on the lips, and it's the kiss is that of a worshipper. "We don't want your staff to hear us. Or maybe we do." He looks at me like a ravenous beast. "So scream, Melanthe. If you really want me to stop, cry out, alarm the staff."

Letting go of my wrists, he moves to my breasts, unleashing his lust. He cups them in his palms that are so big they feel like the paws of a beast, a low rumble in his chest. His lips part as he feels my breasts, my nipples hardening in his hands so much they hurt.

I want to protest, to scream to prove my point, but I can't bring myself to. I could say that it's just my body acting of its own accord, having been starved of connection for so long, but I'd be lying to myself. I offer myself completely into his touch. I wish I could at least not make sounds, save some face, but I sigh at the sensation of him gently massaging my breasts like he worships them. Those hands that explore my body could squash me so easily it's scary, but that only adds to this forbidden excitement.

God, how he touches my long-neglected body. I've been so terrified of being needy, that I avoided even acknowledging my needs. I actually never really had purely *sexual* needs, which is probably understandable considering the heavy brick of a secret that I've been carrying around all my life, but now I discover I might have *sensual* needs. And now, as Achilles Wolf's hands play my body, I realize just how much my body has craved this.

He caresses the sides of my torso like the hands of a blind musician feeling a violin. Both musician and violin vibrate with the energy between them, with the possibility of the music they could make together.

"Will you scream?" His voice comes out thickened with lust. "Do you still want to be saved?"

I respond by arching my body into his hands, lifting my arms up along the wall like a stretching cat.

"Ah, Melanthe," he hisses. The way my name comes out of his mouth moves chords inside me that I didn't even know existed.

He bends into a deep kiss again, our mouths like two magnets pulling each other in with a force neither of us can fight. And at this point, neither of us wants to. The part of me that should be screaming to stop, screaming that this is insane, preposterous, even sick, is just watching like a guilty accomplice. It remains silent even as Achilles slides two fingers between my folds through my pubic hair, discovering how heavily wet I am for him. I take in a sharp breath, my nipples so hard it's painful, the skin on my breasts pebbling.

He loves my nipples with his tongue, circling and sucking like he's getting dirty with ice cream.

"Melanthe, you have the tits of a goddess." He cups them with his fingers, like one would cup delicate flowers. In truth, his hands look like weapons compared to my small breasts.

I giggle, another thing I don't remember when I've done last. Achilles comes back up to full height and looks down at my face, breathing in my scent off his fingers. I stare fascinated as he does it, and can't help imagining him eating my pussy.

But what he does is bring his fingers to my lips. They open of their own accord as he touches them, slipping his fingers inside my mouth. Instinctively, I suck, shamelessly giving him bedroom eyes. God, what's wrong with me? He awakens things inside me that have no business in the heart of a frigid widow.

He clenches his jaw, his teeth gritting as I suck on those strong fingers that feel like stones, and that taste of me. I suck them to his knuckles, holding his inflamed stare, daring him to push me to my knees and give it to my mouth. Yes, this beast, I imagine him fucking my mouth, debasing this frigid councilwoman who dares suck him like a wanton. But what he does is take his hand away and stick those two fingers inside my crack, pushing through my tight walls.

I flinch, grabbing his shoulders.

"Easy," I tell him, releasing the truth through my teeth. "It's been a long time since anyone has been down there."

"How long?"

My chest is flushed, and the air in my lungs hot, but there's no mistaking the jealousy in the way he said that. The interesting thing is, that instead of upsetting me, it makes me even hornier. A corner of my mouth quirks up.

"Does it matter right now?"

"Yes, it does." He curls his fingers deeper inside of me. I may not have the experience he thinks, but I understand he's making a point, exercising his control over my body. An excited sense of rebellion increases the burn under my skin, one that I find refreshingly pleasant instead of infuriating. I always hated the idea of a man stating his ownership over me, it inflamed me in ways nothing else did, but with him, things are different. I kind of like it.

"Everything that happened in your private life could be a lead to the serpents," he says. "Some of your lovers could have even *been* serpents. How many lovers did you even have? Who was the last one? Was it Murray? Then it can't have been *that* long since you've last—"

"Don't cross that line, not unless you want things to go bad." I try to dismount his hand, but he hooks it in deeper. I hiss, my walls clenching around him, but not in discomfort, on the fucking contrary.

"If we're intimate enough to be naked with each other, then we're intimate enough to talk about these things," he says through his teeth, his mouth close to my face.

I just defy him with my stare for a few moments, calling on all the strength of my character to deal with this. No better time to let the shrew inside me take the reins. "First of all, I'm the only one who's naked here, and I didn't invite any of this. Things just...happened. How about we stop."

His yellow eyes are ablaze, and for a moment I'm afraid he's going to step away from me, but he doesn't.

"How long have you been with Murray?" he presses on.

"Achilles, let. Me. Go."

"I told you—you want me off of you, scream."

"What for? It's not like anyone could do anything about this." I look him up and down to make a point.

"I wouldn't dream of hurting anyone in this house. But you alerting them, that's the, say, safe word, to me."

He resumes working his hand inside me, while holding my gaze captive. I try to resist, but I can't, and release a moan as his fingers move with the fluidity of an expert. I gasp as he finds my sweet spot, both my hands clamping on his forearm. But when I feel those sinews moving underneath his tattooed skin, my clit starts throbbing violently, and I come in his hand. It's a long orgasm, longer than I ever gave myself using my hand. Must be because he's an expert at this.

But for me, it's a completely new thing when more pleasure blasts from that spot he found deep inside. I can feel my whole face distort as I scream, my hands clenching on his wrist with all my strength, but he's so strong I can't make him loosen up. I can't gain any control over the sensations he's giving me. My toes curl, and my flesh shivers on my bones.

The sounds I make as I come are as unappealing as my face must be. I sound more like I'm being exorcized than like I'm having the first deep orgasm of my life, at forty-eight years of age. I anticipate that I'm going to feel like shit when I come down from the climax, but the look in Achilles' face doesn't suggest amusement or that he's in any way repelled by my expression of pleasure. On the contrary, he's thirsty to take it in, he's watching my face relentlessly.

His fingers move slower, and gentler, allowing me to recover from the highs that only he has ever taken me. I know from romance novels that I should be feeling dizzy, not even fully sure of what has just happened, but it's nothing like that for me. I know full well what just happened—Achilles Wolf has just given me a mind-blowing orgasm. And I just found out that the G-spot isn't only fantasy.

He eases his hand out of me, his eyes leaving my face and sliding down to my heaving chest, my pussy, and my legs.

And now what do I do with myself? What do I— Oh, God...

He brings his hand to his mouth, breathes in deeply, and licks my juice off his fingers. I stare with an open mouth, wanting to rip that shirt off of him, and lick the wolf tattoo whose tail coils over his pectoral. That shirt hugs his body, hinting at that powerful frame, and I can barely keep the drool in my mouth.

"Melanthe."

Fuck. I was too loud. I screamed my pleasure not caring if the world went down in flames, and someone heard. Murray heard. Wait, Murray is back?

Achilles whirls around, his back broadening as he shields me behind him, while I snatch the towel from the floor. Jesus Christ, I got caught naked with him.

I walk around Achilles, keeping the towel around me and stopping between him and Murray.

"There is an explanation for this," I manage.

"I..." Murray babbles, staring like he's stumped. "I'm back, I—"

But before he can finish Achilles' hand snaps around his neck, the yellow in his eyes ignited.

"What the hell is this?" he rumbles, sniffing at poor Murray like a wolf at a bloody piece of meat. "You. It was you the whole time."

Achilles

IT WAS THE CHAUFFEUR. It was his scent that I've been sniffing on the air the whole day. It got gradually stronger because he was on his way back. I circle him, sniffing at him like an attack dog.

"Where have you been? Because it wasn't only where I sent you. And whom have you been with? Don't even try to lie."

He reddens to the tips of his ears, his pulse skyrocketing, but when Melanthe exchanges that look with him, a sinking feeling hits my stomach. I can't help myself, and grab her arm, yanking her to me.

"You know where he's been. You know he's had to do with serpents."

"Let go, you brute, you're hurting me," she orders. The Melanthe I first met is back. The woman who spent her night in the chauffeur's arms, that night which returns to me like the memory of a trauma, striking me in the head.

"You treacherous wench," I spew through my teeth, wishing I could lock myself with her in her room and force her to tell me everything, as if that could also force her to never want another man except me. Fuck, I have never wanted to force myself into a woman's life like this. Why do I want to force myself into hers no matter the price? I want it so badly that I spew venom at them both, more out of jealousy than in a genuine search for truth, even I'm aware of that.

"You were in with the serpents all this time, weren't you?" I press, even though I can see in her eyes that I'm making matters worse. "And you know more about your husband's death than you let on, but the charade is now over. I will get the truth, if I have to pummel him for it." I grab the chauffeur's shirt, and twist it in my fist. It takes great control not to punch a hole straight through his ribcage, but I manage to remind myself that getting information is more important than unloading my jealous rage.

"It's not what you think, let him go," Melanthe cries, throwing herself at us, practically hanging herself on my arm.

"Whatever either of you says right now, let it be the truth, because otherwise things will get ugly."

"They're not exactly pretty right now either," Melanthe manages as my hand loosens from the chauffeur. He pats his chest as if he can't believe he's still alive, then looks up at me with the big eyes of a lamb. I'd normally pity such a creature, but not when I remember how his hands traveled under the silky sheets all over Melanthe's body.

I back him into a corner, where he stumbles and falls right onto his ass.

"I couldn't identify the smell this morning because it wasn't only serpent reek. It was the smell of an acolyte—a human hosting one of those vipers—paired with human. It was someone who—" I breathe in, closing my eyes so I can identify the unique mix of smells perfectly. "Someone who you exchanged sweat with. Sweat and saliva, and other body fluids." My eyes snap open as I identify that last one. Cum. Male cum. "Wait a minute. You had sex with *a man*?"

My eyes dart to Melanthe, all kinds of ideas popping up in my head. Wait a minute, what's going on here?

"You really need to work on your temper," Melanthe says, looking daggers at me.

"You knew? And you were sleeping with him anyway?"

The anger in her eyes intensifies to the point that they glow like jewels. "Just how thick are you, Achilles?" She slides on a bathrobe and goes over to the chauffeur, helping him off the floor. There's kinship in the way she does it, in the care of her touch as she grabs his arm. Something binds them that's deeper than sex or lust, and that raises more anxiety in my chest, because I don't know if it's better or worse than what I feared. But at least the need to punch him senseless is gone.

"Murray has been my only friend for years," Melanthe explains. "There's nothing sexual between us, and I'm not going to say another word about our relationship."

Relief washes over me, but fuck, along with it comes the realization of what I've done. I went too far, I was too brusque with her, and almost made marmalade of the chauffeur's face. I reach for her.

"Melanthe."

"No." She yanks her hand away before I can grab it, and places it gently on Murray's chest that I abused only a minute ago.

"I'm sorry, but please try to understand," I say softly. "His smell mingled with that of a serpent acolyte. I've been tracing that smell all day, been trying to keep you safe from whatever it was out there, and now that I knew what it was, I..."

"You know damn well what this was. The serpents weren't why you went ballistic on Murray."

"He still has to explain what he was doing with an acolyte. This is a serious thing under the circumstances." I frown at the chauffeur. He swallows hard, as if the physical contact between us finally helped him realize what he's up against. "You smell of serpent acolyte, and you better explain how the fuck that happened, because it's not the kind of business that I sent you out with."

"No," he finally says. "But you kept sending me out on jobs that didn't really mean anything, you just." He swallows, reassessing whether he should say it or not, but he goes for it in the end. "You just wanted me away from Melanthe. You wanted to take away from her anyone who provided some emotional support, make her crack and admit that she had something to do with Charles' death. But I assure you, she didn't."

"Did *you*?" I jerk my chin at him, making a point about his smell, about him hanging out with serpents.

"I'm not *with* them. Look, I met someone, okay?" He opens his arms in an I'm-done-hiding gesture. "He was—I don't know, you kept sending me on these meaningless jobs in Silverdale, I just." He looks down, shaking his head, biting his lips, too distressed to go on. I narrow my eyes. I'll be damned, the chauffeur is in love. "I didn't know he was an acolyte, okay? I'm not even sure he knows what's nesting inside him."

He looks up at me with big eyes. "If you're right, and there's a bred viper in his body, will it—" He hesitates, as if he's afraid of the answer. "Will it kill him, in the end?"

The more I look at him, the more my anger subsides, and I end up feeling for him. I'd put a hand on his shoulder, but when I make a move to do so, Melanthe draws closer to him protectively.

"Will it, Achilles?" she asks when I take too long to answer. But I'm sure she can see it in my eyes. She turns to him, changing to subject to shift his attention.

"Oh, my, Murray, I didn't even get to call you and let you know. I have big news. I got Charles' seat in the Council," she announces, her pitch high as she tries to distract Murray from the subject. But his eyes still hang on me for a few long moments before he turns to her.

"I'm sorry, Melanthe, but I don't give a fuck about your seat in the Council right now. I didn't know that Dane was an acolyte. I spent a lifetime looking for someone like him, and the idea that he could die, it's—"

"Murray." She grabs his face, but it's almost a slap. "I hate making things about myself right now, but if we want to do something for Dane and others like him, we need to act against the serpents, and we need to do it quick. And the first step is discovering as quickly as possible who they have the Council, who is making things possible for them in Darkwood Falls. Our first and best chance to do that is tonight at the pub, so we better get ready." She glances at me, and goes on. "There will be a lot of security there. Why don't you bring Dane over? At least that way he'll be safe, and under *some* expert supervision if the viper inside him starts acting up."

"No way that's going to happen."

The green in Melanthe's irises flashing with power, and the semi in my pants strains painfully. This willful woman is mine, I imprinted on her, and there's no way out of it for either of us. Only she doesn't know it yet.

"If that man doesn't know that he's been used as a host for a serpent, he needs protection. We can't just know what's happening to him and do nothing about it."

"Our job is to protect Darkwood Falls, Melanthe. Right now, the borders are closed, no one gets in, no one gets out. Until the serpents have been defeated for good, we won't provide protection for any outsiders."

She raises her chin, squares her shoulders, suddenly seeming larger than life. I stop talking, remembering how vulnerable she was in my arms only minutes ago. How I experienced a part of her that no one has in... maybe never. There are stories that wolves touch something in their mates that would otherwise remain dormant forever.

Now that I know there's nothing between her and Murray, and my jealous madness is resting with its snout on its paws, I see that what she told me about not having been with a man in many years could really be the truth. But there's no point trying to fool myself. I see how I could easily slip into that other extreme in which I'd keep her locked in an ivory tower, simply because I couldn't bear the thought of any guy even fantasizing about her, let alone touching her.

"Listen Achilles, I understand you and your brothers have to focus on this town, because Fated Females are a commodity that serpents will put up one hell of a fight for. As a councilwoman, I even support that, I support you prioritizing the people of this town. But that's easier on our morals when the people outside of our protective circles don't have names and faces. In this case, we have a name. Dane. Dane is a man who doesn't know that the serpents have inoculated him."

"We don't know that." I glance at Murray. I don't want to hurt him, but there's no other way. "He could have slithered his way into your life *in order to* infiltrate Darkwood Falls. Otherwise, why would the serpents even be interested in him, why choose him of all people to inoculate?"

The chauffeur shifts his weight from one leg to the other impatiently. My eyes turn to slits.

"Listen, Murray, you're gonna have to be very honest about this relationship of yours, because if you're not telling us everything, it could cost many people in Darkwood Falls their lives."

His chin trembles like he could cry, even though he tries to keep it down. "If I tell you who he is, it will only lower the chances that you'll save him."

"His chances aren't great as it is."

"Okay, fine." He chews on the inside of his cheek while both Melanthe and I give him our attention. "He's the son of the town's mayor. No one there knows he is... well, like me, that he likes men. He's already started a political career in Silverdale, and if the truth came out—" He doesn't have to finish. We both know, Melanthe and I, and one look at each other confirms that. "His father on the other hand, he may well be in with the serpents. He never liked me coming around—allegedly I'm Dane's former college mate. He thinks I'm a bad influence simply because I come from Darkwood Falls. Not to mention that, as a chauffeur, I'm much beneath his standing."

I rest a hand on his shoulder, and this time, Melanthe lets me.

"Then he's probably how the serpents keep his father compliant, and it will be harder to get him within the protection of Darkwood Falls than it would for a normal person."

"Please." Tears shimmer in the chauffeur's eyes.

"Achilles, you have to understand," Murray insists, his voice breaking over tears. "I know it was the worst time for me to fall in love, I'm well aware of that. But believe me, there was no standing in the way of those feelings as they came rolling over Dane and me like an avalanche."

I look at Melanthe. Had he said those words a few hours ago, before I imprinted on her, turning her from a Fated Female into my bonded mate, they might not have had the same impact. Or would they have? If I'm honest, I've been interested in Melanthe from the start, I just managed to reject the idea at first. I was able to shove the attraction under the carpet and pretend it wasn't there. But I knew from the start that she was special.

The first night I watched her in bed with Murray irritated me to the point that I couldn't see reason anymore, and I kept giving myself all sorts of meaningless explanations for that. I blamed my irritation on my suspicions that she might have arranged her ex-husband's death, but now I can't deny that I was fighting the chemistry between us.

"Fine. I'll see what I can do, but I'll have to discuss it with my brothers first."

"No, don't." The chauffeur reacts grabs my hand. My eyes turn to slits in an instant, but I don't back away. "They won't want to hear of it."

"There's no way I'm letting a viper infected outsider secretly into our midst," I decree in a cutting tone. "Especially not without Nero's knowledge."

"Come on, Achilles, we all know you don't depend on him for decisions like this."

I step into his private space, causing him to let go of my wrist and back off. There's an urgency in his eyes that I fear might be induced by his lover. I'm more convinced by the second that this Dane guy is using the chauffeur's love for him to make it past our defenses.

"Actually, you might find more understanding for your situation with Nero than with me. He is the mayor of this town, and he's had direct dealings with Silverdale's City Hall. Whatever he decides, gets done."

Achilles

NERO RUBS HIS CHIN as he listens to my account about the love story between Melanthe's chauffeur and the son of Silverdale's mayor. He's sitting in the leather armchair by the fireplace in his house, wearing an open shirt, and the smell of his mate all over him. Luckily Princess has been feeling better these past few weeks, and by the smell in here, it had to do with a lot of fucking.

"I think we should let him in," he says in the end. My brows shoot up to my hairline.

"Did you listen to a word I said after the sob story? The chauffeur insists that we bring an inoculated guy into Darkwood Falls without your knowledge. Doesn't that set off alarms for you?"

"He might well be acting out the shadow councilman's schemes, even the Reaper's, that's true, but think about it." He leans forward, elbows on his knees. "Letting him in, and making the serpents feel like they've won might well work in our favor. They'll get giddy, and they'll make mistakes."

"So what you're saying is let the guy in, make him feel like we trust him?"

"Yes, and keep close tabs on him. Watch his every move, even where his eyes are moving, who he's getting close to without even talking to them. He could try to send notes underhand and stuff like that."

"That sounds like the eighties. Nowadays people can communicate on the dark web, you know."

Nero leans back in his seat, and I drop onto the sofa, rubbing my face with both hands, running them over my three-days worth of beard. I imagine Melanthe moaning as I pleasure her with my mouth, wearing this beard.

"We should have Hercules do it. I'm still busy with Melanthe, and it looks like I'll be busy with her for a while now."

Nero's wolf eyes zero in on mine when I say that.

"You were actually supposed to get off the job tomorrow. Have you started to enjoy it or what?"

I keep staring at the fireplace, my heart beating faster as I think about telling my brother what happened. Telling him that my life has changed forever. It's more awkward for me than it was for him, or even Conan, because until I took this job as Melanthe's bodyguard I was a daredevil who enjoyed his freedom and a wild lifestyle fucking rich women for information. I have the reputation of a Casanova, which has been something of a business card so far.

"This will come as a shock, but it happened, Nero," I say, so low that it would be only mumbling to human ears. "I found my bonded mate."

Nero's brow furrows, as if he's not sure what he's hearing at first. "You imprinted on someone?"

I nod, my eyes fixed on the cold fireplace. I can't bring myself to look at him. I mean, I know he'd never laugh in my face, but I also know that's what I deserve. After how much I've mocked him and Conan, and especially Drago when he imprinted on a woman he'd been hired to fuck for money, I deserve to be held up to ridicule.

But, like I expected, Nero is too much of a wise ass to do that. He stands and comes over, sinking slowly into the couch by my side, staring ahead, just like me, and avoiding eye contact. It helps a lot that he's not looking at me, and he knows it.

"And who is it?"

Okay, preparing to launch the nuke. "I don't know how to tell you. I'm not sure how you'll react."

"Why would I react in any way but with heartfelt congratulations?"

"You really don't imagine why?" And I leave it at that. I can actually feel the air thicken as Nero finally understands. He turns his head slowly, as if in tune with the realization.

"You've gotta be shitting me," he says. "Melanthe?"

I nod.

"But. How can that—? What the fuck, Achilles?"

Us wolves have seen a lot in your lives, which means few things can still surprise us. I mean, the fuck. We were born to filthy rich parents, top one percent in Europe five hundred years ago, and when they died, we got thrown into an orphanage that resembled a jail. Jails and orphanages were hell back in the day, so my brothers and I have been steeled against all kinds of shit. But even we've got to admit that two brothers falling for mother and daughter is a whole new level of fucked up.

"How did it happen?"

"We were in the car together. It was right after the Council accepted that she took over her late husband's seat. I was taking her home to prepare for the celebration at the pub—another weird thing, if you ask me. I mean, why would the town's aristocrats prepare a celebration for one of their own at the town's pub? I know it's the most popular place in town, but still."

"Don't try to derail me. How did you end up imprinting on Melanthe Skye out of all the women in Darkwood Falls? I mean, you kind of fucked all of them."

"Some on your orders."

"That's beside the point."

I nod, returning to the story, replaying it in my head. "I was... I was staring at her in the rearview mirror, and we almost collided with another car, and—"

"Wait a minute, did we jump to *after* you imprinted on her?"

"No, that was before."

"That's strange, isn't it? You losing your focus on driving because you were staring at a woman that wasn't yet your bonded mate."

I rub my hands together, feeling the yellow in my irises intensify as I let it go through my head. The woman has had me distracted for a while now. The more I think about it, the more I fear that I was hers long before the connection struck.

"She needed to calm down," I continue. Recounting what happened helps me put order in my thoughts. "So, I pulled over, I accompanied her through a breathing session, we started talking, we connected. It felt as if, even though she'd resented my presence in her life up to that moment, especially since I kept sending Murray away, in that moment she saw me differently. Almost like a friend."

"A zone you would have probably got stuck in if she didn't secretly feel attracted to you," Nero reasons. "You wouldn't have been able to imprint on a woman that didn't want you at all."

"She acted like she despised me, but I could sometimes smell her arousal. Something she was very good at suppressing. No other woman I know has been able to deny herself like that. She did it so well, I don't even think she was aware of it. I don't think she even knew that she was feeling horny." I get up and pace the room as I speak. It helps me deal with it better. "When she told me that she hadn't been with a man in a long time, I didn't believe her, but actually it makes sense. The problem was that the idea of her belonging to someone else was enough to irritate me so much it itched, and I refused to believe it. But her ability to remain so cold, to suppress her needs, Nero, think about it." I spin on my heel. "It's something we saw before, in the girls we saved in war zones, girls that have been through serious trauma. That's exactly the kind of coldness that I'd been seeing in Melanthe until, well, until it happened."

"Go on," he says.

I rub my forehead with my hand. "Then I blew it. There was something about another guy, and I think I got jealous. She got mad at me, and then I caught this scent on the air, the one I've been telling you about all day on the phone. It got so strong I felt threat was near. We got in the car, I drove like a madman, and then she leaned forward, between the front seats. We looked at each other and..." I stop at the window, staring out at the sky. "The world went up in flames."

Actually, what happened is that she became my world.

I keep staring out the window, exploring this new music these ancient chords make. They're like vestigial muscles that I never used before, but now that they've been activated, what they do is mind-blowing. All the sex I've had with other women has become meaningless. What happened today, with her, even though it didn't go all the way, it meant the world. It was almost like a wedding.

"So where does it go from here, Nero?" I ask with a strange sense of anguish. "What do I do? Because let's be honest, it's not like I can just go and propose, like Drago did with Arianna, you with Princess, and Conan with Janine."

The leather sofa squeaks as Nero stands.

"No," he says like a doctor who must keep calm while delivering deadly news. "It would be social suicide for her here in Darkwood Falls to start something with you. Not to mention that she would probably lose everything she has."

Oh, don't I know that.

"On the other hand," he says, "it's not in the wolves' nature *not* to act on this bond. Actually, with every day that passes without claiming her, it's going to be harder to control yourself."

"So what do I do?"

He stops by my side, pushing his hands into the pockets of his jeans and staring out at his front terrace, and the sky. We're shoulder to shoulder again.

"So she is the woman I smell on you."

The statement puts a knot in my throat. Had it been any other affair I would have talked about it without any shame, but this is Melanthe. *My* Melanthe. Luckily, my silence is answer enough for Nero. I know that he's feeling awkward, too, because, in the end, he's fucking the daughter while I'm dying to fuck the mother, and I would totally fuck her senseless, if I had my way. But this one detail I have to give him. He needs it if I want him to help me.

"We didn't go all the way, Melanthe and I, today. It was...something else."

"I can't believe I'm asking this, but what happened exactly?"

"We were in her room, we were talking, she was getting ready for a bath. At a certain point I couldn't hear her anymore. It was like I was talking to myself. So I went to her closet, and there she was, completely naked, and I think... I think she was touching herself. The moment I saw her naked I was floored. The whole world got sucked away, and there was only her. And me. Only the two of us. She was mortified, of course, and she ran over to the bathroom, turned on the water, but the die had been cast, and there was no turning back. I was attracted to her like a magnet, I just needed, I—"

"I understand," Nero says in an attempt to make it easier on me.

"It was only me, pleasuring her. I didn't claim her."

"Which was a very smart thing to do. With our bonded mates, things are exactly the other way around than they are with other women. Once we have them, we only crave them more. It's a two-way street, too. Once they have us, they can't breathe without us either. It's what ensures that both partners have their emotional needs met over the course of the years."

"Speaking of years." I look at him, arching an eyebrow. "I'm sure you noticed how young Melanthe looks. It's almost unnatural."

Nero shrugs. "It's not unusual for women like her to look half their age. She is rich, well connected, she was active in the fashion world."

"Yeah, but those women usually have surgeries and special diets and personal trainers and whatnot, while Melanthe, everything is natural on her." No need to point out again how I know that for sure.

"Achilles, Princess and I have talked a lot about her mother, and she never mentioned anything supernatural going on with Melanthe. The supernatural entered their lives the moment we did. It all started with Drago and Arianna."

"Actually, it started with Sullivan, the former mayor and Arianna's ex. The serpents had been here for a long time, for generations, they had just been hiding extremely well."

"So what exactly are you saying?"

"I'm saying that maybe Melanthe has been touched by serpent business in some way, without her even knowing."

Nero crosses his arms over his chest, letting this go through his head.

"We need to find out exactly how Charles Skye was involved with the serpents, and we'll dive into Melanthe's past as we go. Thing is, only Melanthe can help us with that. Another reason why you should keep your connection with her under wraps."

"But that's exactly it, how do I do that, Nero? Damn it, help me. I need you more than I ever did in all these years."

He takes a few moments and gabs my shoulders. "Look at it this way—your attentions can only hurt Melanthe, at least at this point."

"By the way things look, there might never come a time for Melanthe and I to be together."

He looks down at his feet, his hands still firm on my shoulders.

"Fuck, Nero, you might as well tell me that I have a deadly disease. Actually, I'd rather that were the case."

"I know you would. But you really have to be strong now, not for yourself but for Melanthe. Just imagine, if you were to act on your feelings. Do you really want to make her that woman who's sleeping with her bodyguard? The Council will tear her apart on that account, they'll take the seat away from her, and everything her late husband left her. They will jump on her like hyenas, they'll rend her, and not only in Darkwood Falls. The people sitting in that Council are dangerous, well-connected angry men that can hurt her so badly she won't find a quiet place anywhere in the United States. As for Princess." He glances over his shoulder, and lowers his voice. "Can you imagine what Princess will think of her? They're not exactly on good terms as it is, and trust me, I tried to plead Melanthe's case, because I always thought she was innocent, and had nothing to do with her ex-husband's death."

"I was suspicious of her, but now I know what was behind it. I wanted to hate her because of how my wolf craved to love her."

"It's in her best interest for you to back off. And the most important thing of all—do not, for the love of God, sleep with her. If you do, you're doomed, both of you."

The silence that falls between us after that last warning is crushing. It knocks the air from my lungs.

"I don't think anything ever hurt more than what you're asking of me right now," I say thickly.

"It's not me asking this of you, it's the situation that demands it. For Melanthe's good. Speaking of which, there's one other thing I've been meaning to talk to you about."

Nero opens his mouth to speak, but before he can say something, the rest of our brothers barge in, almost knocking down the door.

"What the fuck, Achilles, you imprinted on Melanthe Skye?" Conan blurts out.

"Lady Cruelle? Princess' *mother*?" Drago follows. "Oh, I wish I could have seen *that* happen."

Fuck, they must have heard the last sentences of my conversation with Nero as they came toward the house. Wolf senses.

Every one of their words is like a dagger plunging into my chest. It's not that it bothers me, them talking like that, on the contrary. I know they mean well in a way few people could even understand, and I wish I could receive their brotherly jackass remarks with a grin. I wish I could smugly take in their slaps on my back, welcoming me into the club of mated wolves, but my situation is different. Fucked up. Cruel.

"Keep it down," Nero warns them. "We don't want Princess to hear. Not yet."

Conan looks back at the stairs that lead up to the house's upper floors, but at this hour I expect Princess to be up in the attic study, working on her journal. According to Nero, her shrink said writing stuff down will help her process what happened with her old man, and so far it's been working.

"Another way in which acting on your feelings for Melanthe would hurt her," Nero says, placing a large hand on my shoulder. "Princess understands bonding, fated mates, fated females and all, she understands better than anyone since she and I had our own challenges, but she won't be rational regarding her mother's love life anytime soon. I'm sorry, brother, I really am."

"Wait a minute, what's happening here?" Drago demands, approaching with Conan like a boxer flanked by a large troll. I know I can always count on them to back me up on any battle, but unfortunately there's nothing they can do about this one.

I wait as Nero explains, trying to tune out his words because I can't bear to hear them again. I drop onto the couch, burying my face in my palms, but I can feel my brothers staring at me when Nero is done.

"There's gotta be something we can do," Drago insists. "Come on, Nero, you know what imprinting means for a wolf. He won't be able to stay away from her forever. He'll be a shell of himself in no time."

"They haven't consummated the bond yet," Nero says. "That will make it somewhat easier."

"Yes, but it will still be torture," Conan protests. He looks even fiercer than usual when he frowns, enhancing the scar that runs down his face from his eyebrow, and the hardness of his features.

"Painful and fucking outrageous," Drago puts in, tightening his fists as if he were getting ready to fight an invisible enemy. "I mean, okay, it's clear that it will take a lot of fighting, but we have to help. We have to find a way to make this happen for them."

Nero's composed nature usually calms down my brothers' wilder spirits, but this time they're too frustrated with the situation, probably as much as I am. They won't stop arguing with Nero, so I guess I have to do this.

"It's all right," I say.

They watch me as I come back to my feet, slowly and heavily, ready to make what will probably be the most difficult decision of my life. "It's a sacrifice I have to make. And I'm willing to make it." I scoff, but the sound is bitter and laden with loss. I don't feel an ounce of my usual lighthearted self in my body anymore. "After all, this relationship would only be a stigma for Melanthe, even if we lived far away from Darkwood Falls. To the world, she would always be the cougar, the MILF with a much younger lover. Her bodyguard, no less. She probably even had her husband killed in order to be with him, that's what they'll say." My throat closes.

"No, Achilles," Drago says, but I've already started towards the door. I slam it behind me, wishing he'd just leave it alone, but he yanks the door open and runs after me onto the terrace. I don't get to reach to the stairs before he grabs my arm and spins me around.

"You're not letting her go, you hear me?" He holds up his fist in my face, his knuckles still like tree bark from all the serpent skulls he crushed in underground fights before he got together with Arianna. "We're gonna find a way to make this happen for the both of you. I'll talk to Arianna, she'll deal with that brat Princess Skye."

"Soon to be Princess Wolf, I may remind you, our alpha's wife."

"Especially because of that she should know better than to stand in the way of your love with Melanthe."

"Listen, Drago, I know you mean well, but I've already made my decision." I square my shoulders, and take a deep breath, determined to face my destiny. "I am letting Melanthe go. It's the best I can do for her, for you, for the entire Darkwood Falls. I'll do everything in my power to free this town of the serpents. And when we finally meet the Reaper, I'll be the one to fight him." Because, without my mate, I'm the only expendable one.

CHAPTER IV

Melanthe

The pub is overly crowded, but Murray still manages to trail after me with a drink in his hand. "So, we really not gonna talk about the elephant in the room?"

"Excuse me?" I say over my shoulder, keeping on meeting people's gazes and nodding as I greet them.

"You and the bodyguard? When I came in, you were, you know—" He leans over my shoulder and whispers so low in my ear that I can feel his breath. "Fucking."

Current runs through my back muscles, turning me stiff as a rod. "We weren't fucking."

"You were completely naked, and he'd backed you up against the wall. Your hot skin, on that cold, tiled wall—"

"Stop."

"Why? Is the picture alone enough to get you wet again?"

"Now that we've got your boyfriend under the protection of the wolves, you think you can turn impertinent on me?"

"Don't get me wrong, Melanthe. I'm just happy for you, super happy actually. I'd lost hope I'd live to see such a thing. You, having an affair."

"I'm not having an affair with Achilles."

"Oh, you're gonna marry him then? Introduce him to your daughter and the Council officially as your new boyfriend? I suspect the answer is no, in which case I'm very curious how you would classify your relationship."

"We don't have a relationship, okay?"

"There she is," an angry, nasal voice interrupts as its owner steps into my way. It's Clayton Ray, of course.

"Clayton," I greet him, holding up my flute of champagne. "I see you freshened up, new suit. It screams Armani from a distance. Too bad there is no brand that can save your face."

"So fresh in your late husband's seat, and already showing your true colors. Spewing venom. But don't sing of victory just yet. The others will soon begin to see whom they've let into our midst," he says, clinking his flute a little too hard against mine.

"Clayton, come on." Tanner Moreno appears behind him. Tall, olive-skinned, with hazel eyes and the lips of Jason Momoa, the upper part of his white shirt open to reveal a virile hairy chest. He's a man with power over women, all right. Power he's trying to use on me now.

In all my years in the world of glamour, I've learnt to recognize the tricks of men who want to pass as casually seductive. Like they're not even trying. But, like Tanner, even the way they walk is a show-off.

There's only one way to deal with this kind of men—use their own tactics against them. I smile, raising my glass, looking at him through the golden, sparkling champagne.

"Thank you for having supported me this whole time, Tanner. You were a big part of this success."

"Indeed, I was."

Clayton glares at him like an angry piglet as Tanner steps proudly between him and me, thus cutting him off. There are other people waiting to talk to me, the pub is full of the finest society in town—a rare occasion for The Big Bad Wolf pub—but Tanner's sense of entitlement blinds him, as it often does.

"It was a close fight, but we made it," he says.

"I'll find a way to repay you for your support as soon as we've eliminated the serpents from the picture, I promise you that. You're my next big focus."

"Oh, Melanthe, you know you don't need to do that." He takes my hand in his, and raises it to his mouth while fixing me with those hazel eyes from under bushy black eyebrows. It's a studied look, with little feeling behind it. "I only made sure you got what was rightfully yours. Charles made it clear in the documents he left behind that he wanted you to take the reins of his businesses, and his seat in the Council. I'm merely making sure that his wishes are respected."

"I know. You are a precious friend, Tanner." I don't emphasize 'friend' enough, because I need his hopes high. It's how I'll start getting the kind of information out of him that I need—all the dirty data on each and every one of the councilmen. It's him that

I got the info on Clayton's wife from, and I know there's plenty more where that came from.

He offers me his arm so that we walk together to greet people. Murray tenses behind me.

"Tanner, with all my love, I must refuse." I arch an eyebrow and sweep the pub with my eyes, making a point. "You know there are people here who would use anything against me, and my—*our*—success is too fresh. Walking on the arm of the most handsome man in the room could have serious consequences, especially on my first day as a councilwoman and custodian of Charles' companies."

"Of course." He takes distance, but he does it with a wink. "No problem. I can be patient."

Good, his hopes are high up there where I need them. I have the advantage because he thinks he's on his way to using me in the future, when in truth I'm already using him. I grin to myself as I start walking among the guests. What Tanner should be smart enough to expect is that I know every trick in the book, and would never fall for someone like him. I see right through him. He's after Charles' wealth and his connections, which he hopes to secure himself a piece of by working his way into my bed.

I'm offended, really, that he should think I'm needy and weak enough to fall for that. To be played by a sexy stud. Unless that sexy stud is Achilles Wolf, the only man that ever touched my sexual chord. He did from the beginning, when I met those animal yellow eyes with my own. From that moment on, I was always aware of him. I was permanently on edge, feeling him around the house, infuriatingly unattainable because I wouldn't let myself even fantasize about him that way, when every part of me screamed to do it.

I sweep the pub for him, but there's no sign of my tall, yellow-eyed Adonis. He brought me here and left me with Murray, saying we had enough wolf protection both inside and outside the pub, and went to see his brothers about the business of Murray's boyfriend. I wanted to help Murray, but truth is, I'm not entirely sure I did the right thing. We're in the middle of an invisible war.

I talk to people, and within the next couple of hours there have been so many that my voice goes rough. Not to mention that my feet are killing me in my stilettoes, and wearing a black corset dress isn't making it particularly easy to breathe. But corset or not, it's not as sexy as Sibyl Ray's dress. She's wearing black, too, a split dress, her milky white leg shooting out of it with every step she takes.

I follow her with my eyes, thinking how I look more like a lady from two centuries ago, the only sexy thing about my outfit being the corset, while she's a young, fresh floozy. One that's heading right towards Achilles.

He's here. My heart leaps into my throat. There he is, by the door, wearing jeans and a black polo shirt that hugs that fighter body. His arm muscles bulge through the long sleeves, and his masculine features seem to glow, making him the most beautiful man in the room, and I'm pretty sure that's not only in my eyes. He looks exactly like a male model that belongs on the covers of magazines, and who sure as hell could never belong to one woman alone. My heart twists, and a sour taste spreads in my mouth.

Sibyl greets him with a wide, bleached smile, her white arms opening wide to hug him. My lips harden, and my nostrils burn like I'm breathing fire. She and Achilles had a brief affair before. She's younger than me, a tart, surely an expert at pleasuring men, while I'm a frigid fish.

Yes, the floozy is everything I'm not. A young version of Monroe, a blonde dream. She married the piglet Clayton a few years ago and, judging by his temper, he hasn't seen much of her pussy lately, which must be because she's kept herself satisfied with Achilles. Well, at least I know for a fact they haven't seen each other these past few weeks, because he's been busy guarding me twenty-four seven.

He bends down to her, and gives her a curt hug. I watch them with slitted eyes, my pulse running wild.

"They haven't seen each other at all this month." Tanner's whisper over my shoulder startles me, because I've been too focused on the two, so much so that I'd tuned out everything around me.

"Which is strange," he says, falling in line with me and watching the two as well. "Because my sources say they'd been banging a lot before he took his position as your bodyguard."

"Yes, I guess I've kept him busy."

He leans into my side, speaking like an accomplice, trying to give me the impression that I can trust him with anything. Even his voice is an invitation to open up. "You were smart to send the chauffeur away these past few weeks. If before that people had a vague suspicion that you were having an affair with him, it died when you kept showing up everywhere without him."

"Really, it had that much of an impact?" I sip the sparkling champagne, my eyes fixed on Achilles and the floozy talking by the door. He keeps glancing at me, more often now that I'm talking to Tanner. He holds a particular dislike for the guy, which I intend to exploit tonight.

"Honestly, it was Achilles' idea to get rid of Murray," I say. "At first I thought he just didn't trust him, but now I understand it was a strategic decision."

"Despite him having been quite the asset for you lately." Tanner angles his body toward me, demanding my attention. "I'd be careful about the wolf, Melanthe. Sybil Ray isn't the only lady in town he's had trysts with. I hear his brother Drago actually was a callboy before he fell for Arianna, and I don't think Achilles is that different from him. He might try to, well, win your favors."

Well, shit. The last thing I need is for this bastard to get wind about Achilles and me.

"Tanner, can I ask a favor?" I say smoothly, hooking an arm around his. "Introduce me to some of those people you told me about. Those that I owe my victory to, the people you influenced in my favor. I would like to thank them personally."

He grins, lines forming on his cheeks from his eyes to his jaw. "Oh, I don't know, Melanthe, love. They're very private, I told you. And only a few are here anyway."

"Please, you have to let me show my gratitude. You know, this kind of people, I'm one of them. We say we don't want any recognition, or that we want to keep our identities in the dark, but secretly, we want nothing more than to be *seen*."

"You know, if you really want to show your gratitude, you can start with me."

My eyebrows shoot up. I may have been a cold fish until a few hours ago when Achilles Wolf rocked my world, but there's no misinterpreting that tone. And his stepping into my private space, lacing his hand with mine, is unbeatable confirmation. I back away.

"Tanner, there are people watching." And among those people, Achilles, who's ignoring the floozy completely and watches us with eyes of murder. Which makes sense, considering Tanner's growing audacity. "Remember what we talked about."

Tanner looks around, as if he's just become aware of our surroundings again. "You're right. I'm forgetting myself. Forgive me, I got carried away." He meets my eyes, and makes my stomach turn. I can see his falsehood so clearly. "I'll leave you to enjoy your evening, and your victory. You've earned it. But before I do, I'd like to confess." He takes a deep breath, making a show of how he's struggling with himself to do this. "I... I have a thing for you, Melanthe. I couldn't stop thinking about you since the moment you stepped into the council room a month ago, as Charles' widow, claiming to be his legal successor in everything. I'd never thought of you that way before because, well, you understand. There was

Charles, and you were frankly hardly ever in Darkwood Falls. But now that I've gotten the chance to know you..." His voice trails off, but his eyes fix me. There's lust in them, I think, but I can't be sure. What I do know is that it's different from Achilles'.

I give him a smile that doesn't reach my eyes. "You're putting me in a delicate situation, Tanner."

"Meet me later," he says, taking my hand. He keeps it down, making the moment secret and therefore all the more intimate.

"I'll find you," I whisper back, wanting nothing but to get him off my case as soon as possible. Achilles' intense stare isn't helping things, my skin burns from it.

Tanner steps away, keeping what he thinks is a seductive grin on his face. He raises his glass and turns around, making his way through the crowd. I breathe out in relief, turning around and bumping into Murray.

"You're gonna have some explaining to do," he says, motioning with his head in Achilles' general direction. "Lover boy over there stared at you the entire time, and he didn't look happy. It looked like he could kill Tanner, and I'm not the only one who noticed."

A glance around the place tells me he's right. People have taken notice of Achilles' reaction to my exchange with Tanner. Men look from him to me with hawkish eyes, while many of the women stare over the rims of their glasses with catty envy that's as familiar to me as Tanner's seductive tactics. Hell, it seems like there's endless competition out there for this man.

My mind starts swirling around one question—How many of these women have had him inside them? How many did he pleasure the way he did me in the bathroom only hours ago? Have I resisted the seductive tactics of men like Tanner all these years only to fall prey to Achilles Wolf's charms that were nothing but sharper skills?

"Congratulations, Councilwoman Skye," a woman's voice tears me from my thoughts. I discover it's none other than Sybil Ray. Damn, her dress is so low cut I can see down to her navel. "The first woman to take a seat in the Council, that's quite an achievement. You're an inspiration."

"Thank you?" It's a question, because it sure as hell didn't sound like real congratulations. She starts pacing around me like someone circling prey, which I'm not used to tolerating. My fingers clench dangerously around the stem of my glass, and I can already visualize myself smashing it right on top of that full head of Marilyn-blonde hair.

"That should keep you busy and safe," she says. "Being a councilwoman and official custodian of all your husband's affairs will require quite a lot of your attention, I imagine." She halts in front of me, pointy chin up. It's obvious she's had her lips done, they resemble red balloons that are about to blow up. I imagine them wrapped around Achilles' cock, and I want to scratch her, so bad. "That should give your bodyguard Achilles Wolf some free time, isn't it? Will you be needing his services at all, now that you'll be surrounded by dozens of other bodyguards?"

Okay, now I see where this is going. I step closer, making good use of the difference in height between Sybil and me.

"The Wolf brothers remain responsible for my security, and Achilles' unique expertise may still be required. But why the interest, Sybil? Because I doubt you want to give him a job. Your husband is not exactly a fan of the Wolf brothers. On the contrary, he was a great supporter of the former mayor Sullivan."

Something foxy crosses her blue eyes. The black eyeliner tail adds to the effect.

"If you're accusing Clayton of having to do with the serpents, I assure you it's not true. He did support Sullivan, yes, but he didn't know what Sullivan was."

"That still doesn't answer my question—why your interest in Achilles?"

Her plumped-up lips thin a little as they draw into a grin. She drifts a little towards the bar, and leans with an elbow against it.

"Okay, you got me. The question was just meant as a cover for my true curiosity—is he your lover?"

I stiffen, thunder cracking through my head at her audacity. I can feel the stem of my flute fissuring between my fingers.

"What could possibly give you that idea?"

"Oh, it's simple." She tries to mask the jealousy crossing her face as she says it, but it's too late. I've seen it. "The way he stares at you the entire time."

"Oh, but of course he stares at me. He's still my bodyguard, and I'm walking freely in the middle of a crowd. It's his job to watch me all the time. In fact, it would be bad news if he took his eyes off of me.

Which, between the two of us, he did when you went over."

"Come on, Melanthe. We're both aware that no woman with blood in her veins would fail to take notice of Achilles Wolf in *that* way. I'll tell you a little secret. Something I wouldn't tell anyone else. If he were my bodyguard, I would have screwed him at least ten times by now."

"Oh, but you screwed him anyway, even though he wasn't working for you."

I might as well have slapped her with these words. She falls back onto a barstool, as if she can't believe what I just said. I grin triumphantly, but I can barely still suppress the need to fist my hand in her hair and bang her head against the bar counter.

"That's preposterous," she manages.

"Listen, Sybil, and listen well, because I'm only going to say this once. I didn't get where I am now—on the Council, and at the helm of Charles' business—by being weak or meek. I may not always look it, but I'm a dangerous woman. You think you're smart and slithery enough to hide well, but make no mistake, there's no hiding from *me*. Fuck him again, and I will find out. I will also tell your husband, if you don't play exactly by the rules I lay out."

This isn't something I do often, but when I do it, I mean it. Sybil stares up at me, her face so red not even the tons of foundation that she's wearing can hide it. She's dying to spit into my face and scream that no one tells her what to do, but she can't afford it and she knows it. The tension between us makes me feel bigger, and her feel smaller, I can tell by the way she cringes on the stool. I give her a crooked smile, and turn on my heel, prancing away from her.

I keep my shoulders back, making my way through the people congratulating me, some stopping me to talk about our future relations, now that my late husband's businesses are in my hands. But I haven't pushed down this fury that Sybil has put in my chest, a fury that works its way up to my throat. I manage to keep my cool enough to assure everyone that my office is going to contact them about our future dealings, and that I'm sure we'll find a way to see them run smoothly.

But all this composure is as fake as it gets. On the inside I'm burning, the veins in my temples pulsing. I don't even notice that Achilles has made his way to me, gripping my upper arm. I want to turn, but I bump with my back into his body. He won't let me.

"You were getting cozy there with Tanner Moreno," he reproaches in a gravelly voice.

"You were having quite the rage with your flame Sybil Ray, too."

"There was no rage."

"But there was a flame."

"It's dangerous for you to be around Tanner. One of the councilmen is in with the serpents, and until we know exactly who it is, you can't trust anyone." He lets go of my arm, and pushes his chest into my back, the sign that I should start walking. The guests' suspicions have already been awakened, we don't want any more of those.

"I assure you, there's no way I'll trust anyone here."

"You can trust my brothers and me, so it's not like you don't have any support."

"What happened with Dane? Have you gotten him over into Darkwood Falls?"

"We got him, but we didn't bring him into town. He's under surveillance at Janine's hotel in the woods. If serpents follow his trail, it's better it doesn't lead into the heart of Darkwood Falls."

"All right. But please get Murray there as soon as possible. He's dying to see his boyfriend."

"Don't change the subject, Melanthe. What did that Tanner guy want from you?"

"Wasn't it obvious? He was hitting on me."

His fingers clamp on my arm, and he spins me around. "Are you playing with me?" he growls through his teeth, his beast rearing its head behind those shining yellow irises. A chill runs down my spine, of fear but also excitement. I've never felt so alive.

"Why do you even care? Your hands were half up that floozy's skirt just minutes ago."

"You know that's not true."

"Oh, no? She came to talk to me, basically to ask me to release you from my service so you'll have more time for her. So tell me Achilles. Are you going to do that when you no longer have to look after me? Will you jump right back into her bed?"

I'm boiling with anger, holding my face up at him, my lips drawn in a hard line, demanding. But he doesn't answer. He actually doesn't deny it. His eyes just roam my face like he could either grab my jaw and kiss me violently, or hurl me over the tables.

A flash of red to my right draws my attention—the only thing that could tear through my focus on Achilles. It's Princess, standing in the door with Nero.

"She came." I whisper, a happy flutter in my heart. "She actually came."

"Good to see that you can express something other than bitterness," Achilles says, sounding harsh. "Too bad there's only room for one in your heart."

He walks away, his shirt molding to the muscles on his back with every move. I keep glancing from him to Princess, who makes her way to me, leaving her husband to greet the councilmen. She stops in front of me, her usually soft, loving hazel eyes unreadable. She doesn't say anything, so I just ramble, dying to fill the space between us.

"Honey. I'm so happy you finally relinquished the black." I look down at her. She's wearing a pencil skirt with a fitted high waist, and a white shirt, as loose on her upper body as her skirt is tight on her legs.

"I thought it was time."

"So you've been feeling better?"

"You mean have I processed dad's death? No, I haven't. I spent years by his side Mom, doing a lot of things that *you* should have done. When you take care of people like that you tend to get so close to them they're basically part of you."

"Aren't I part of you, too?" I have serious trouble keeping the tears from my voice. I've lived through so much shit, and navigated my way through such terrible people that nothing can really tear me down anymore, but she is my soft spot. The adversities of life made me stronger, but nothing can prepare a mother for her child's resentment.

"You've been too absent from my life, Mom."

"I was there as much as I could be."

"No. Not as much as you could be. And sure as hell not enough." I can see she wants to cry, too, but, like me, she holds it in.

Turns out my daughter is stronger than me. I try hard not to fall apart right here, in front of my enemies. I'm aware of everyone watching me, especially Achilles.

"I only came here because Nero asked me to," Princess concludes. "Because if I had my way, I wouldn't have come. I can't bring myself to forgive you, Mom. I can't help feeling that, if you'd been there for Dad all these years, he wouldn't have deteriorated the way he did, and maybe, just maybe he'd still be alive."

"I understand." I make to take her hand in mine, but she doesn't respond to the gesture, so I drop it. I give her a smile filled with all the love I feel for her. "You can't force yourself to feel what you don't, and I didn't raise you to do that. I fought for your freedom when no other girl was allowed to leave Darkwood Falls, and I won't be the one to restrict it now. You go ahead and bathe in those feelings of resentment for as long as you need to. And when, and *if* you ever find an ounce of love for me in your heart, I'll be the happiest mother in the world. Until then, I'll always be there if you need me. Even if what you need is to scream, to yell, to accuse, to hurt. I'll take it all."

I better get out of here before my enemies get a huge boost in satisfaction through watching me fall apart right here in their midst. I manage to keep a stiff back and a straight face as I make my way towards the back of the pub, ignoring the wolves that try to stop me.

"Ma'am, the back veranda is off limits," one of the Italians says.

"Get out of my way, pretty boy," I grumble. He hesitates, but then he moves to the side. It must be obvious by the look on my face that I'm not to be messed with, not today.

I emerge into the crispy evening air, closing my eyes and taking in a few deep breaths to calm down the pulsing pain in my chest. It felt like dying in there. Part of me wished I did. I open my eyes to take in the night. There are so many stars scattered in the sky, they're like glitter on a canopy of rich black velvet. I raise my hand, convinced that, if I try hard enough, I can reach them.

God, I need a place where I can let go. Where I can let this façade of toughness crack, and curl up with a thick, fluffy pillow. Or maybe with someone I love for a change. I wish I could have loved more people in my life. Maybe if I'd had more children, even if it was with Charles Skye. I find a wooden bench by the wall and lower myself tiredly on it, staring at the dark forest in front of me. Wind rustles through the trees, making the dark peaks of their crowns sway. It's so dark but for the glitter in the sky, that shapes and contours in the black is all I can make out.

I lean my head back against the wooden wall, thankful for the darkness and smell of fir. I brace myself, wishing it were the arms of someone else. A specific someone, not some dream lover. I wish for Achilles. I listen to the breeze rustle softly through the trees, but it's not just the breeze. I hear something else behind it, too.

I sit up straight on the bench, hands in my lap. I must look like a possum listening for danger, training my ears on that strange sound. It's low, but clear enough that I can identify it as something different, and it seems like it's picking up, too. It's a swooshing sound, like something slithering through the grass.

Multiple somethings. I stand and walk slowly to the wooden banister of the veranda, curiosity winning over fear, a curse I've been carrying around forever. I freeze in terror when I discover dozens of silvery snakes in the grass, making their way towards me. I take a deep breath and scream with all I have, but I can't move an inch. I'm petrified here, my hands on the banister, watching dozens of little animals crawling up to me.

This must be a nightmare. The more I scream, the less able I am to move, until strong hands pick me up, and move me out of the way. The next thing I know, Achilles' broad back blocks the snakes from my sight. He throws off his polo shirt, cracks his knuckles, and moves his head from side to side, getting ready for battle. What happens next feels surreal.

Fur sprouts all over his body, his bones growing with deafening cracking sounds, his muscles inflating. I stumble backwards, falling with my upper body inside the pub's corridor, and my legs still out on the veranda. I watch Achilles shift right before my eyes. His fingers morph into black claws, so sharp that they glint in the light, looking like blades. He opens his arms as power runs through him, howling at the moon, the sound raising goose bumps all over my skin. I can't believe this is all really happening.

Snakes creep onto the wooden ledge of the banister, opening their mouths to reveal cobra fangs, hissing and growing bigger by the second. It's like they're feeding from some invisible sources. One of them throws itself at Achilles so swiftly that I have no doubt it's going to stick its fangs right into his face. But I can only see him from the back, his bluish-black fur with its metallic sheen giving him an indestructible polish.

He intercepts the snake in the air, slashes at it with his claws, and its body falls in pieces on the ground with meaty thuds. The floor shakes as men run towards us from the pub. Two of them leap over me, and as they do, I can see their stomachs as they shift in the air. It's Nero and Conan, erupting from their skin into the enlarged shapes of their fearsome wolves.

They land flanking their brother, stomping and squashing the serpents, while Achilles cuts the snakes into pieces, his bulging bluish-black arms moving so fast they seem a blur. But soon the serpents starting growing, becoming so big within seconds they're the size of men. Two of them coil viciously around Achilles' arms, keeping them apart and exposing him to the other serpents that fly at him like arrows.

I scream with all I've got, which triggers Achilles. He flexes his arms, throwing himself backwards to the ground, the serpents hissing and disentangling from his arms. Achilles gets heavily back to his feet, but more serpents throw themselves at him. My heart hammers against my chest, but my mind is paralyzed as the snakes move past Nero and Conan where they are engaged with a number of serpents already. They slither towards me, their split tongues fluttering out. My skin crawls, and I start scrambling backwards, failing to get up to my feet. The snakes are too many. I'm not going to make it out of this alive. They'll coil around me, squeeze, choke me to death.

Only they don't. The moment the first one tenses its scaly body to leap at me, Achilles' deadly claw snaps around it right under its head, making a horrible squelching sound. The snake's face freezes in terror, and when Achilles lets go, it hits the wooden floor in two pieces that resemble two sausages butchered at one end. My stomach leaps into my throat, and I just can't resist the urge to vomit. I lean to the side and throw up right here on the floor, a pressure behind my eyes that makes them tear.

I hear muffled commotion in the background, people screaming, fire, I smell smoke. The fire is all around me sooner than I expect it, but when a powerful, furry arm scoops me off the floor and swings me over the beast's shoulder, I understand it's Achilles. His hard wolf muscles push into my stomach, making me want to throw up again, but I manage to hold it, desperate just to get out of here.

The serpents hiss and twist, and I realize the fire didn't start itself—the wolves set it. The flames lick dangerously close to my body, and the smoke filling my lungs. I haven't fainted in a long time, but I definitely will any moment now. I manage to resist until Achilles emerges with me on the other side of the pub, but when he puts me on the ground, my face hot and aglow from the fire that consumes the building we just escaped from, my heart stops, and my eyes almost pop out of my skull.

Never in my life have I seen something as fierce as his face. This is the first time I have seen him up close. In his wolf form, even if it's humanoid, like in those movies with the Lycans, Achilles is a real beast. He's got fangs as sharp as metal, and electric eyes that send current zapping all through me. The blood drains from my head, and I fall limp on the ground.

CHAPTER V

Melanthe

The first thing I know when I come back to my senses, is that antique furniture is spinning around me. The room is large, very large, like a palace ballroom. I lift myself heavily off whatever it is that I'm lying on. What I know is that it's hard as stone. Putting a hand to my head, I look to the side to discover I'd been resting on Achilles chest, while he's sitting on a baroque sofa that's too lumpy to be comfortable. Achilles the man, this time.

"How the hell—where are we? What happened?"

Achilles is wearing an open white shirt that's clearly not his because it's not large enough for the sides to meet across his chest. It reveals a lot of his tattooed body, on which I had been lying, a lump of unfulfilled desire forms in my throat. The jeans and the boots he's wearing must belong to one of his brothers', two of whom are here, because I can hear them talking, even though the sound is still muffled. My senses are still not completely re-sharpened, the only thing I'm sharply aware Achilles' presence.

I force myself to look away from him, turning my attention to this large room that resembles that of a

European museum castle, with windows that remind me of a gothic cathedral. I know the place, that I've been here before, but I can't put my finger on it. Where do I know it from? I narrow my eyes, trying to remember. That's when the other two wolves' words become clear.

"If they got here, it means they took the hotel." That's Hercules, a colossus of a man with torn clothes. Hercules is the biggest of the Wolf brothers, as muscular as a Mr. Olympia. He's something circus directors would have advertised heavily back in the day.

"I just talked to Drago," Nero says. "He and Conan were able to bring Janine and Dane safely to Drago's place. They're now with Arianna and the cubs. The chauffeur made it to the house too, and the two lover boys are now happily united. The rest of us though." They keep talking about how they secured the town, and are still holding the serpents at bay—the serpents who have come here in throngs for Dane—but they don't mention the one name I'm desperate to hear.

"Christ, where is Princess?" I yelp, jumping to my feet. I get dizzy immediately, and fall back against Achilles', who stood up to catch me.

Nero's head snaps to me.

"Melanthe, you recovered. How do you feel?" he says, heading over. Achilles' arms close protectively around my waist from behind. I know he does it for support, but I can't help but give in to his almost-embrace in search of comfort. I crave it the way a freezing human craves a hearth. I look up at his face, and a flash of the wolf that caused me to faint lights up in my head. I stiffen in his hold, but I don't try to escape it. How the hell can I feel such paradoxical things at the same time? I'm scared of him, but I wouldn't get away from him if I had a choice.

But then someone else comes to greet me, and bile rises in my throat.

"Melanthe, you're awake," the floozy states in her annoying, impossible voice. She doesn't manage to sound quite as concerned as she intended. The way her eyes slit when she sees Achilles' arms around me doesn't leave much room for interpretations.

He lets go of me immediately, however. I'm instantly cold, and so angry I could scratch them both, but I pace myself.

"Tell me where she is, Nero," I say. "Where is Princess?"

He holds up his hand, his tone soothing.

"She is fine. She's at Drago and Arianna's place. We're at councilman Clayton Ray's, who was kind enough to offer his house for the protection of everyone at the pub. It was closest. The town is under serpent siege."

"Clayton Ray *helped*?" It doesn't make any sense. I'm ninety-nine percent sure he was the one helping the serpents.

"We managed to save everyone from the pub, and kill all the snakes with fire," Achilles takes over. "But people were scared, chaotic, and well." He looks at Sybil, and shrugs. "We needed all the help we could get. Clayton reacted quickly, and he and his people helped us gather everyone here."

"And we'll all stay here until the serpents are completely eliminated," Nero concludes.

"Eliminated." I scoff. "Okay, I was passed out for most of what happened, but I did experience that first attack at the pub. It was the serpents that cornered us. I'm far from an expert on conflict management, but even a child knows there's no winning a battle from a corner."

Hercules folds those humungous arms over his chest, smiling at Nero, who seems strangely sure of himself, too. I look up at Achilles again, seeking confirmation. He must see things my way. But the handsome features of his face are like carved stone. Sure, he doesn't want his lover to get the wrong idea, like that he might care about me. God, how I want to hurt them both, especially him. Her, I can understand, really. Even I, as a cold fish, have lost my head for this stud. What can one expect from the young wife of a councilman who resembles a rosy pig on the best of days.

"We have been preparing for this for a long time," Nero explains. "We expected it, we expected that the serpents would come if we removed Dane from Silverdale and brought him here. They managed to breach the town, but we curtailed that. Still, now we have to play the prey, and wait." His eyes sweep over the large room, and I understand that he can't say more in front of all the people here.

Now I realize that there are more people here than I originally registered. What happened at the pub shook me hard, and I'm still recovering. I sit back down on the antique cushioned sofa.

"So now we wait," I repeat, stealing a glance up at Achilles, but I address Nero. "I wish I could be with Princess. Is there no way I can be transferred to Drago's house?"

Sybil snorts, stepping closer to Achilles. A growl forms in my throat, and my nose creases like that of a hissing cat, but I get a grip.

"Really, even in a desperate situation like this one, all you can think about is yourself? And how do you imagine that the distinguished councilwoman will get escorted from one house to another? We are on the other side of town, Melanthe! People have been ordered to stay inside their homes. Wolf squads are patrolling everywhere, do you really expect them to make an extra effort now and move you over to your sweet little daughter?"

"Sybil, please," Achilles says. "She didn't make any demands, she just asked if it was possible."

"She was thinking of herself!"

"No, you stupid bimbo, I was thinking of my daughter!"

Rage twists Sibyl's heart-shaped face, and for a moment she stops resembling Marilyn Monroe, and instead takes the semblance of a boar. She snaps at me, and I stand in a split second, ready to meet her, but Achilles wraps an arm around her waist and pulls her back.

"Let me go, I'll teach her!" she screams, and I'm dying to let her have it, but Achilles places himself between us.

"I suggest you go get a grip, Sybil. This isn't the time or the place for personal problems."

He puts her down, but she tries to come at me again, which prompts him to intercept her and drag her away. I'm ready to go after them and deal with the floozy once and for all, but guess who else is here, and slides into my field of vision. It's Tanner, with a broad, white smile that almost blinds me.

"I would say that destiny has a plan for us," he drawls, and it makes my ears bleed. I really hate the way this guy talks. "You and I, in the same shelter."

My eyes rake over him.

"You're in pretty good shape." His clothes, too. "Weren't you there when the fire broke out?"

"I was out for some fresh air, so I was spared the shock."

I look around the room. He seems to be the only one who was spared. There are more people here than I originally assessed, scattered all over, and they're all in pretty bad shape. I spot many pairs of eyes on us. They probably saw when Achilles' arms were around me, too. Incredible how they still hunger for gossip, even though they look like they've just escaped a bombing. Some of Clayton's staff run around, offering blankets and hot beverages, and the aristocrats accept them with the attitude of kings and queens, even though they look like beggars.

"This place looks like a refugee camp," I say.

"It's what it is at the moment. The fire at the pub was quite the experience for everybody here, and it will probably remain a trauma for most of them. But hey." He takes my face in his palms, a sudden and unwelcome gesture. "You were attacked by snakes.

That must have been terrible." He searches my eyes as if he wants to see the whole thing in them.

"Achilles stepped in at the last moment." I step back, pushing his hands down from my face. I look past him at Nero and Hercules, wanting to get there and ask the details of their future plans, but they're focused on their own discussion, and Tanner doesn't seem willing to let go.

"Melanthe, now really? Do you feel safe with them? I mean, despite their protection, the snakes got to you. You should see yourself, you look like a ghost."

"I feel like one, too."

I become increasingly aware of myself, but I'm still distracted. But it's not only the shock of the snakes' attack. It's this place, this palace. I've been here before, but not with Charles, not in the context of a socialites' event, or a simple visit. No, it was something else, but no matter how hard I try, I can't seem to remember.

"Come on, let's take you upstairs. Clayton prepared a few rooms for the council people so they can rest and freshen up," Tanner says secretively in my ear, putting an arm around me. It feels strong and dependable, but it's not Achilles' arm, and that enrages me. I shake it off, and when Tanner stares at me with wide eyes and an open mouth, surprised by the vehemence of my rejection, I manage a trembling smile.

"I'm sorry. It's what happened at the pub. I just can't get it out of my head. Every touch feels like a threat."

"All right," he says, though his tone is a bit harsh. "I've said it before, I'll be patient. But remember, Melanthe, we're in this together, we need to stay close and learn to trust each other. And we need to learn it quickly. As you can see, we can't rely on the wolves, they're not as able to keep us safe as they'd have us believe."

He leads me towards the exit along the wall, in order to keep us both as inconspicuous as possible. The bastard is wearing perfume, musk and tobacco, while all the others look like hell. I'm pretty damn sure he wasn't outside the pub when it happened. He must have run out first to save his own ass, and then he must have been the first who took advantage of Clayton's hospitality for the councilmen, and gotten cleaned up.

Clayton. I don't trust him, and I need to talk to Nero, Hercules, or even Achilles about it.

Tanner takes me out into a large but dimly lit corridor with a large staircase that leads up to the upper levels of the house. Suddenly my vision warps, and I lose balance. I can't fall, because Tanner has got me, but it's like a door has been kicked open. I remember more. I narrow my eyes, trying to scrutinize my memory, penetrate into its dark recesses. I grip the medallion hanging form a chain around my neck.

"I've been here before," I breathe.

"Of course you have, you've visited Clayton with Charles, I'm sure."

"No, Charles and I never attended any events here."

"I'm sure you have, Sybil likes hosting at least six a year."

"Clayton has only been with Sybil for five years. I haven't been here for most of that time."

"Melanthe, you really need to rest. That's why you're getting these ideas. Come on," he says, in a tone that urges me to snap out of it, and move away from the subject, but I don't want to. I tear myself from his arms, going towards the staircase, my eyes on the blurry window above the first landing, the shell-shaped one. I take the first steps, and make out the figures talking in the corner of the landing. I move faster, discovering that the two people are Achilles and Sybil. Their heads are close together, but it's obvious they're only talking—for the time being. Her hand lands on his chest, sliding down between his naked pectorals and along his abs.

Rage takes over me. This feeling hits me that he is mine alone, that he belongs to me, and that Sybil is seriously trespassing.

I take the stairs faster, making sure they can hear me. Sybil turns around, her eyes flashing wickedly as she recognizes me.

"Melanthe," she spits.

I stalk over with my shoulders back, ignoring Tanner's calls. I stop right in front of them, and meet Achilles' eyes. He looks calm, but at the same time there's something tense in his expression, like he's focused on something. I glance down at his jeans, desperate to know whether Sybil had an effect on him, even though I manage to hide that desperation. To my relief, it doesn't look like she had.

"Achilles, a word."

Sybil places her hands on her hips, ready to defy me, but Achilles puts a hand lightly on her shoulder, causing her to move away.

"Please. We won't be long. I'm still officially her bodyguard."

She still seems unwilling, but I feel triumphant, even if only for a second.

"Tanner was going to show me to the *privileged* rooms," I tell her. "Why don't you go with him and find someone else that would like to take advantage of that privilege. I relinquish mine."

Tanner protests, but I'm not even listening to him, locking eyes with Achilles and feeling how fire courses all through me. All I care about is setting the record straight with him, which is what I'm going to do at the end of this conversation.

Achilles watches the two as they reluctantly leave us, and I can actually feel Sybil's jealous eyes on me as she turns to look at us over her shoulder.

"You should be more careful about how you approach me. People can't wait to get ideas." Achilles hooks his thumbs into the pockets of his jeans, and I can't help myself. My eyes slide down his chest to his abs, his bronze skin glowing in the light from the shell window. He's so damn handsome that the detached way he speaks to me hurts like red iron.

"Don't worry," I reply bitterly. "I have no intention of approaching you more than is necessary."

He waits patiently for me to get to the point, but I can read nothing beyond that in his face. It's like he couldn't care less about me on a personal level.

"Why are we trusting Clayton all of a sudden? Wasn't he high up on your list when it came to who might have had Charles killed, and who helped the serpents? We might all be sitting ducks."

"We're not."

"How can you be sure? You didn't expect the serpents to corner us the way they did, and you were wrong. They came dangerously close to killing us all. What makes you think you're not wrong this time?"

"I can't disclose that now. Is there danger still out there? Yes. But I assure you, my brothers and I are on this one hundred percent, and if anyone is going to lose their lives, it's going to be us, and not one of the town's people. All you have to do is take care of yourself, and stay away from—" He glances over my head, and I know immediately what he means. "People whose loyalties we are not yet certain of."

I scoff. The nerve of him. "I'd take no issue with that if I didn't seriously doubt your people reading skills." I look him up and down in a way that I mean to be contemptuous, but I'm afraid rather pathetic. "You are having an affair with a woman of highly questionable morals, and you seem to be enjoying it. Not that it bothers me. You're free to do whatever you please, with whomever you want. But I won't take your opinion about people very seriously, thank you very much."

He cocks an eyebrow, and for a moment his temper shows.

"You seemed pretty busy with Tanner, too. It's not just my opinion that he's shady, everybody knows that."

"Tanner isn't on the suspect list."

"Everyone is on the suspect list."

"He helped me with my so-called campaign to get the seat in the council. If he were with the serpents, he wouldn't have done that."

"You know damn well he had his own agenda for helping you, whether he's the serpents' man or not."

"If you're so convinced that was his only motivation, why are you so concerned about my closeness to him?"

"You talk as if I were jealous of the guy, Melanthe. I assure you, that's not the case. I'm wary of him."

That cuts like a knife through my heart, and my throat constricts. There's the truth of it, then.

"Here's what I'd do in your place," he continues, closing the space between us that's scarce anyway. He towers over me, pushing out that perfectly chiseled jaw. "If you must keep Tanner around you, I'd use the chance to make progress. Find out who it was that betrayed your husband and helped the serpents in. I have a hunch that Tanner will lead you close to the answer if you give him, you know, that kind of attention. Leave the rest to me and my brothers."

It's not the finality of his words that gets to me, but the finality of his tone. I nod, grateful for all the fury that pools in my chest, this urge to 'show him'. To hurt him. It also makes me painfully aware of how badly I want him. In the end, this was the first man who showed me that I was, against all odds, still a sexual being.

I turn my back on Achilles Wolf, and walk proudly back the way I came. A piece of my heart breaks with every step, but what doesn't kill me will make me stronger.

Achilles

FUCK THAT. I KNOW SHE wants to get back at me for hurting her, but she's getting too damn close to Tanner. I thought I'd be able to put up with this, but fuck, I'm not. He grows bold in putting his hands on her, and she doesn't reject him. As for him, I don't think his interest in her is still only material and political. It's turning into an obsession. Like mine.

"It won't stop hurting if you don't stop watching," Nero says. He just got off the phone with Princess. It's painful to watch how he's missing her. If it weren't for the mission, he'd probably melt on his feet without her.

"Thing is, I'm not even sure it hurts," I grunt as I watch them by the well in the garden. I'm sitting on the ledge of the high gothic window, playing the communication gadgets between my fingers. Nero yanks them from my hands.

"Leave those, you're gonna end up destroying them," he says. "We need to get ready. Drago says we got the Reaper right where we need him. He thinks he's got us cornered, with Darkwood Falls under his siege. He's drained Silverdale of serpents, and he's marching them all over here, which gives the Brigade of the Wolves the chance to take over Silverdale and overthrow the serpents there. Cinzia and her lovers have brought more of the Italians. If we're lucky, the Reaper will be confident enough he can win this, and he'll be leading his own armies. That's when we'll trap him between Silverdale and Darkwood Falls, and crush him and his forces once and for all."

There's excitement in his words that he keeps under control like ember. He still thinks we're gonna be fighting the Reaper together. But I'm going to fight him alone. When the time comes, I'll leave town, infiltrate his army, and get him in his camp when he least expects it. I haven't repeated this plan since last time we met because my brothers would never accept the idea, and I don't want to raise their suspicions. But the decision is made, and watching Melanthe with that hairy bastard with vestigial Italian accent only strengthens me.

Living on would mean watching her with him and probably multiple other men. I will never again be an option to her after the way I treated her a few nights ago, which was my purpose. I wanted to push her away, make her resent me, even hate me. But my heart twists in my chest like a stabbed snake, and jealousy is consuming me. This is harder than I thought. I imagine grabbing him by the throat right in front of her, and looking her in the eye as I snap it, and let his body fall limp to the ground.

"This need to make it clear to Melanthe and everyone else that she belongs only to me," I say to Nero, my eyes like a stalker's on Melanthe and Tanner. "It can't be a healthy thing. Did you have it with Princess, too?"

"I still have it, only that it's tame now. Princess does belong to me, and she barely has anything to do with other men, and not because I restricted her in that sense. She just... doesn't need anyone else. It's what happens when one comes together with their bonded mate, things just fall into place, and everyone is happy. But the intensity is always there. Even the insanity. And it's not always easy to manage."

Fuck, I need to channel some of that insanity somehow. I thought that keeping away from her would do the trick, but fuck, it didn't. On the contrary, it pooled in me to the point that I'm about to burst with it. The frustration, the rage when he touches the small of her back like that. They're still by the well beyond the large driveway, with the statues of naked nymphs carrying amphorae on their shoulders from where water used to spout only a week ago. Now we have blocked all the major piping in order to keep the serpents at bay, and to make sure they can't invade the place the way they invaded the Skye manor months ago.

Something snaps in my hands. I look down to discover it was my phone. My knuckles are white, and so much force flows through my arms I'm afraid I'm gonna tear apart whatever falls in my hands next.

"Nero, can you—," I mutter, realizing I won't be able to deal with this alone. But Nero holds up his hand as his smart watch vibrates.

He takes the call and walks away, leaving me alone with the storm in my chest. I look out the window again. At least she's not *entirely* alone with Tanner. There are others strolling through the garden, and while everyone studies them from the corners of their eyes, I don't think they're suspecting an affair.

"Still watching over her." It's Sybil, standing where Nero stood moments ago.

"It's my job. I'm still her bodyguard."

"But she's not your exclusive responsibility anymore, is she?" She nestles in the other corner of the window, sitting on the ledge, her back against the frame. She doesn't have enough room, and I don't intend to make it easy for her. I keep my foot on the ledge, resting my elbow on my knee, but she doesn't get the hint. On the contrary, she lets her eyes graze down my chest. I have to be ready to shift any second, so all I've been wearing have been open jackets over my naked chest, and jeans and boots that I can quickly lose.

"It still hasn't been discussed," I say coldly. "So until we have a plan in place for her, I'm gonna have to keep watching over her."

"But why? She's not in the same danger anymore. All everybody's doing here is lounging around, waiting for the next thing to happen. All access to the house has been blocked, no one gets in or out."

"The entire town was sealed off when the serpents crept behind the pub and attacked her. She's high up on their list of targets. She needs extra attention, Sybil, whether we like it or not."

"To be honest, it doesn't look like you *don't* like it." It's the first time I hear suspicion in her voice, but I'm sure it was there before.

"Sybil, I never meant to ask you this, but I'm curious." I give her a crooked grin, my head leaned against the stony window frame, offering her a sight I know she likes. She told me the night we met that she had a soft spot for well-built men with tattoos and three-day-beards that look at her like smug bastards.

"Why did you marry Clayton? Because it's obvious it wasn't for love, must be obvious to him, too."

She gives me an inviting smile.

"Come on, Achilles, you already know why."

"I wanna hear it from you."

She gestures at everything around us.

"It was the money, of course. I mean look at all this place. When a man of his means sets his eyes on a girl, she better be sure not to miss it."

"That would make perfect sense if you were *any* girl, except you're not." My irises heat up as I activate my wolf vision to scan her for signs of lying. "You come from a long line of rich merchants. You never needed the money."

And there it is. Her pulse changes, her chemistry shifts. I'm on to something.

She smiles, trying to shift my attention. She pulls her knees up to her chest, then rests one against the window, and lowers the other to the side, allowing me to see the flimsy thong between her legs. She's wearing a transparent dress that seems frayed at the hem, and a denim jacket over it. She pushes the sides apart enough for me to see her hard nipples through the dress, but there's absolutely no reaction from my body. I grit my teeth, because that only confirms I'm fucked. I'm never gonna desire another woman besides Melanthe Skye. Yeah, it's probably for the best that I take myself down along with the Reaper.

"How about I tell you more about that tonight? Our usual spot?" Which is a washroom under the grand stairs, but not even the memory of our times there arouses me. I force a smile.

"Curiosity is going to kill me until then."

"Will it?" Her hand slips between her legs, but before I'm even tempted to look, a strange force pulls at me from the side, like a strange kind of energy. I turn my head in its direction to see Melanthe staring right at us from the well, where she's sitting with Tanner. He's got his hand over hers, and when our eyes lock, she places her free hand over his. Hot fury balls behind my eyes. If looks could kill, that fucker would be writhing on the ground now.

"Stop that, Sybil," I grunt. "People are watching. And this is the worst moment of all for your husband to find out about us."

"Ahh," she says as if my words were honey. "Finally you admit there is an us. I'll be waiting for you tonight." She stands, swaying by me and stroking me under my chin with the same finger she's slid through her pussy. My nose wrinkles, but I keep my face away from her so she can't see. "Same time. Don't be late."

Sybil's exit is a relief, but Melanthe's cold glare plunges through my rib cage like a dagger. Her gaze is that of an Ice Queen, as if I'm nothing but a worthless worm to her. Nero said it's impossible for her not to respond to my feelings, since the bond has been created between us, but I have a very hard time believing that.

I push myself off the window frame and stomp towards the corridor, and from there into the place we now call the 'control room', where Nero, our team and I handle the security and monitor the premises. Nero is still on the phone, watching the screens together with

133

Clayton Ray's security people. But all eyes dart over to me when my fist rams into the wall, and bits of concrete hit the floor.

Melanthe

IT'S HAPPENED EVERY night since I can remember. The waking up in the middle of the night, going to the kitchen and having a glass of milk, resting against the counter and looking up at the moon. It gives me a feeling a tranquility that I only get late at night, but it only lasts until I go back to bed. Anxiety grips me by the throat on the way, all the time. And still, I do it every night, the same pattern.

But tonight is different. As I head back to the room I share here on the ground floor with one of the town's elderly ladies—she chose to room with me because I was willing to help her with her baths and her meals—a strange sound stops me in my tracks. I come to a halt.

Moonlight filters through the large shell-shaped window above the landing on the first flight of the grand stairs. Every time I see it my heart hurts. This is where Achilles made it clear to me that I meant nothing to him, while he meant the world to me. I ascribe it to the fact that he was the first to offer me sensual pleasure, and therefore made his way deep into my heart. So deep that tearing him out will hurt so bad it will be impossible to actually do it. I throw poisonous resentment over the feeling. It's all I can do.

There's that sound again, and my skin crawls. I step out of my slippers and follow the creaking, putting one foot in front of the other carefully.

Something is going on inside the washroom under the stairs.

I should go, run and find Achilles or Nero or Conan, tell them there's someone or something in the washroom, but what if they'll be gone by then? What if behind that door is the traitor we've all been looking for, preparing the entrance for the serpents? I could be losing precious moments if I turn my back now like a coward. I only have to get close enough to listen at the door.

This door, the washroom, like the shell-shaped window, I know it. I've been here before. My heart rhythm increases with every step I take until my blood slams so hard through my veins, I'm shaking. The memory that I've been trying so hard to access all this time reveals itself, and I fall like Alice through the rabbit hole. I'm just about to turn the knob when a strong hand wraps around my wrist and pulls me back.

"Melanthe, no." It's Achilles voice, deep and familiar.

"It was here," I blabber. "It was right here, this is where it happened."

"What are you talking about?"

"Just let me, let me, I need to go in." But those impossibly strong hands keep me back.

"No, Sybil is in there, waiting for me," he hisses. I freeze, which only makes it easy for him to sling me over his shoulder and carry me out of there.

But it's too late, the memory is taking me over with a vengeance, even as we speed deeper into the darkness of this place. I think the darkness helps actually, it helps bring back the memory, especially now that we're finally at the place where it all happened.

I've always known what happened to me that night all those years ago, but I'd severely suppressed the details. I always remembered that Charles got the custody when my parents died. As my mother's brother, he was the only family member with a legitimate right to take over her part of my grandparents' goods and properties, *and* her daughter. As for that washroom, the details, they start flashing through my mind like evil pixies.

I grab my head, scrunching my eyes shut against the sharp headache that shoots through my head as Achilles takes me further to the back of the house, away from the staff rooms on the ground, one of which I myself am occupying with the elderly lady. Soon we emerge into the crisp night air, and from there into a small building adjacent to the house, which turns out to be the chapel.

He takes me to the front, where there's more light, and sets me down on a bench. God, how I'm shaking. The moonlight filters through the chapel windows, but Achilles goes to the altar and comes back with a candelabra that sheds a pleasant golden light over his face. He sits down next to me, the wooden bench complaining under his weight. He places the candelabra on the floor in front of us, and searches my eyes like a doctor examining a patient.

"What just happened back there?" His voice is soft, meant to calm me down, and damn it, it's working. The truth comes out of me, the brick that I've been carrying inside my chest for years dissolving with every word that leaves my mouth.

"Charles was my uncle, Achilles. He got custody after my parents died, and he fucked me." I point in the general direction of where we came from, my finger shaking. "Right in there, where you found me, that's where he fucked me for the first time. It went on for years, wherever he could get me, until I got pregnant with Princess, and he married me before it could show. I was twelve the first time," I blabber.

For all his initial composure, Achilles looks stricken now, his yellow eyes wide, his perfect jaw slack. He raises his big hand and strokes my hair, then he cups the side of my face, just like you'd comfort a child. Only an hour ago I would have slapped his hand off of me, but not now. Everything inside me welcomes his warmth. It does me so good that, for the first time in forever, I release the tears, eyes hanging on his. On some weird level, this feels perfect. Like he's the only person in the world that I could have ever opened up to about my terrible secret.

"This house, I knew that I'd been here before since I woke up in it. But I could have never imagined that it was my parents' house. It's where I was born, and where I grew up. But because of Charles' abuse, I wiped it from my memory entirely. The only thing I could remember was that washroom."

"What else do you remember, Melanthe?" He inquires carefully.

"I don't want to remember anything, really. It hurts."

"But you've come this far. If you close the door on it again, you might never find your way back to the truth."

He's right. Not to mention that I feel there's another truth, buried right beneath this one, that's just within my reach and yet I can't grab it.

"What I feel about this house, it's so dark. And this dark feeling, I had it before Charles." I look up above the altar doors as flashes of memory come at me.

"I was sitting right on this bench," I say, my voice the whisper of a ghost. "My mother, she was sitting next to me. My father, next to her. And next to my father." I scrunch my eyes shut, forcing myself to zero in on his face. "Tall, lean, and creepy, sort of a slenderman." Hardly my way of putting things, but it's the most accurate description I can give. "He had a bald head, and green eyes full of, of.... of evil." My eyes snap open.

"My father," I breathe. "He was not my real father. This man was. The slenderman."

"Did you know him? Can you try to remember his name?"

I try to feel my way back to the answers. "He'd been around for a while. Charles knew him, too." I strain for the information, but it just won't come back to me. What I do understand, is that the man sitting next to my supposed father was my real father. My mom had told me that, in great secret, and she said it was a great honor.

"This man. Have you seen him anywhere else except here, in this house, when you were a child?"

I shake my head no. "I think I used to see a lot of him back then, but not since Charles got custody. Achilles, I have a terrible suspicion."

I nestle into his chest, and he wraps his strong, dependable arms around me. A feeling of pure love extends from my stomach to my chest, spreading heat to the rest of my body. It gives me pause, and snaps me right out of this. I push him lightly only enough to look up at his face. What on earth is this? This connection?

And the way he looks at me, like he understands exactly what I'm going through, and it hurts him to watch it. There's a kinship and compassion in his yellow eyes that's far from what one would expect from a beautiful player with the world at his feet. There's a depth of feeling that only an old soul could have. Or someone who loves deeply.

But no. I'm fooling myself again, and I won't let it happen.

"Sybil was in that washroom, waiting for you," I say as I force myself to see the truth behind my delusions. "And you were there for her."

He doesn't deny or confirm, allowing me to draw my own conclusions. Bile rises in my throat. He even stares at me like it pains him to hurt me with that confession. I force a smile, and pull away. I let my eyes rake over him, but God, I can't deny how painfully handsome he is. What I really want is to slide my hands under his leather jacket, feel that steel body, because he belongs to me. I want to throw my arms around his neck and press my lips to his chest, breathe in his scent, and convince myself that what happened between us back at the manor meant something to him as well. But the knowledge that it didn't strikes with a vengeance. It hurts so badly that I could crumble, but I manage to keep on a thin mask of dignity.

"You should go, then. If she misses you for too long she might come looking." I stand, ready to go, because I don't know how long I'll be able to keep up the charade. He stands, too, catching my hands.

"You can't go back alone."

"I'll take the candelabra with me. I'll be fine, I'll find my way." I bend down for it, but Achilles catches me by my shoulders, stopping me. Our eyes meet, and I already know. It's going to happen. He's going to kiss me. He's gonna put that sculpted mouth on mine, simply because he can't help himself. He wants it so badly that it burns him, I can see it in his eyes, and that's no delusion.

Then it happens, and my heart slams against my chest, ready to ram a hole right through it. I should reject him, remind him angrily of the way he rejected me, but instead I abandon myself in his embrace. I respond to his kiss, tilting my face up, making it even easier on him. The fresh scent of his body and his hair mixes with the scent of the leather jacket, awakening my senses. My clit reacts, my pores opening like flowers to take in the sensation of his hands wandering up my arms to my shoulders.

He pushes the satin robe off my shoulders, leaving me completely naked other than my black panties. My skin pebbles in the chill of the chapel, and my nipples harden. God, the idea alone that this werewolf that was out for a rendezvous with another woman is undressing me in a chapel awakens a forbidden excitement inside me. The scandal of it.

I step back, breaking the kiss, and bending down for my robe. I bundle it against my chest and hold it there like a shield as I back away. I just can't give in to these emotions, to this magnetic pull.

"No, Achilles. I'm not that kind of woman. To me, there is no casual sex. Go and have your fun with Sybil, she will let you fuck her every hole. But I won't let you do to me what you did last time."

I turn away, determined to run from him, but he grabs me by my arms, and this time roughly. He spins me around, and wraps his large hand on my jaw.

"You're not going anywhere, Melanthe," he growls, his yellow eyes glowing. I can see the beast rearing its head, that fierce wolf I glimpsed after he fought off the serpents. "I thought I could let you go, I thought I could stay away until the day I met my fate, the Reaper, and went down with him. But I can't. If I am to make this sacrifice, then I might at least taste the forbidden fruit."

He plunges into a kiss, a deep, almost violent one. My blood runs so fast I go dizzy. I can't believe this, did he just say...? I try to pull away, ask for explanations, inspect his face and make sense of the ferocity I saw in it, but he sinks his teeth into my lower lip. I yelp, but he suppresses the sound with his mouth. He parts my lips with his, and pushes his tongue inside my mouth, kissing me with so much passion that it can't be just carnal. This is more, this is an emotional need, one that I respond to entirely.

Every inch of my body craves to merge with his, but the question keeps returning to my head...

I lean back, managing to disengage my lips from his enough to speak up.

"You were coming to that washroom in order to fuck another woman, how can you claim now that—"

"Fuck damn it, Melanthe, I wasn't there for her," he blurts out. "I was there for you."

"For me? But—"

"You've been wandering every night, since the day I met you. Around midnight, you get up, you to the kitchen, you get a glass of milk. You stare up at the sky, your face turning peaceful, and so youthful you barely look a day over twenty-five." His stare deepens, and I see beyond this pained passion that he seems to feel for me and that makes me so happy I could fly. I see the bond between us.

It hits me, and the blood drains from my head.

"Achilles you...you imprinted on me?"

His fingers splay over my naked back, pressing my breast against his rock hard chest, the sides of his leather jacket folding over me.

"It wasn't my choice. It just happened. I wouldn't have done this to you, to me, to either of us if I could've helped it." He presses me so hard against his body it squeezes the air from my lungs, but I don't want him to let go. I don't even try to keep a straight face anymore, all I know is that I want him to keep talking.

"I've been stalking you, Melanthe. I know it's bad, and that we're forbidden, but I can't live like this anymore. And since I don't have much time left anyway, I might as well give in to this madness, at least once."

"Wait, what do you mean—" He closes his mouth over mine before I can finish, his lips hard, and hot, and wet. He keeps me plastered to him with one hand, the other travelling down my back and slipping into my panties from behind, cupping my ass.

I moan into his mouth, my body jerking into his, asking for more of his manly touch. God, I want this man. I want to do things to him I shouldn't even be thinking about. But before I know it, I've started to lower myself, slowly, so he won't try to keep me up, my eyes hanging on his, communicating what I'm going to do. When he understands my intention he grabs me under my armpits.

"Melanthe, no. I'd never let you—"

"Achilles, please," I whisper. "I want to do this. Never in my life have I craved such things." It's perverted, it's something I never even imagined I'd ever want, but here I am. I want to feel you all the way to the back of my throat," I say huskily, my naked knees touching the cold, stone floor. I hook my fingers into the waistband of his jeans, and start popping the buttons open.

I can tell that he still wants to protest, but somehow he can't bring himself to. I have no idea what I'm doing, because I've never sucked a cock, but I know I want to choke on his.

I finally open his jeans, reach in, and free his erection. I'll be damned. This is a weapon, it's so big. I stroke him appreciatively with my fingers, then with both my hands. He twitches in my grasp, hard and wanting, the rush of blood turning the head purple. He's a magnificent beast, but also a man, a virile man whose cock is raging for me.

I don't know where to begin, so I rise on my knees and bring my breasts to the level of his cock, trapping him between them, and moving slowly along his length. I look up at his face to weigh his reaction, but the passion I find in his eyes splinters all my barriers, and I don't care about what this looks like anymore. I'll do exactly what I want to, no matter how outrageous it is.

I bend down and lick his balls. He hisses and flinches, but I stick out my tongue and stroke again, then suck his balls inside my mouth, causing him to flinch. I have no idea where this need to do all kinds of dirty things with him is coming from, but I know that it grows by the second. By the time I open my mouth to take his cock into my mouth, my pussy is soaking wet. I squirm against my panties as my fingers hook into his belt, and I slide down to the root of his cock, taking him in to the back of my throat.

Tears push into my eyes, but I manage to open my throat and take the crest in deeper, my throat swelling.

"Fuck, Melanthe, what are you, ah." He throws his head back and then looks down at me again, his handsome face scrunched as if the pleasure borders on pain. God, the dirty things I want to do with this man. I suck back and forth, with force, wanting to feel him throbbing against my tongue, and then intending to let go in time for his sperm to hit my face. But whatever the sensations I'm causing him, it's too much, and he pulls back, cupping my face.

"God, Melanthe." He bends down and kisses me, his tongue plunging into my mouth. I must be the dirtiest wanton that ever lived, feeling so turned on by the fact that I'm naked, on my knees in front of my bodyguard, sucking his cock in an abandoned chapel. I've spent all my life thinking of myself as a cold fish, only to discover there was a dirty whore inside of me—one that needed true emotional intimacy in order to come to life. I might be a whore, but I'm his whore, and his alone.

I massage his balls while he kisses me, getting better at it. He can't resist in the end, and shoots back, pushing his pelvis forward and literally rubbing his balls in my face.

"Oh, Melanthe, what you're doing to me," he growls, not minding the volume of his voice anymore. Soon he's pushed his cock inside my mouth, holding my head, and fucking my mouth until he comes.

I'd never thought there would come a day when I'd swallow a man's sperm, especially not my bodyguard's, but here I am, doing just that and loving it. And as Achilles Wolf pours his semen down my throat, roaring with pleasure, I come in my panties.

"Who would have thought, huh," I say as I get up to my feet, wiping my mouth, my knees burning. "That Melanthe Skye, the coldest woman that ever existed, would love nothing more than to submit to a wolf man." I caress his jaw, then rise up to my tiptoes, and lick its stubbled contour, the prickle travelling from my tongue, to my navel, to my clit. "To her bonded mate."

Achilles

I LOOK DOWN AT HER impossibly young face. The beautiful Melanthe Skye is mine to love, mine to fuck, mine to own. I can't believe I've just had that full head of red curls between my legs, my cock in her mouth. It was an experience I can't compare to anything.

But now I want more. Much more.

I grab her and swirl her around, bending her over the bench. I'm gonna have all of this forbidden fruit, have its juice flow decadently down my chin, I'm gonna get dirty as fuck with it.

I hold her wrists pinned against her lower back with one hand, and I lower myself to stroke her crack with my tongue. She flinches, but I stroke again, reaching between her labia and flicking my tongue over her clit. But I want to kiss all of her pussy, I want the inside of it, I want the taste of her innermost climax, and I wouldn't be able to control myself if I wanted to. I plunge my tongue into her pussy, fucking her with it, my ears relishing her moans. I keep her wrists locked with one hand, the other firmly clamped on her ass, noticing the perfectly shaved crevice between her cheeks.

Damn, I crave even more intimacy with this woman, I want levels of it that will sure as fuck scare her, but there's no going back now, not for me. I lick her pucker, and when she tries to struggle against it, I clamp my grip down on her wrists, keeping her there, and pushing my tongue inside her ass.

"Achilles, what on earth, ah, lord," she cries, but I respond but pushing deeper, fucking her ass with my tongue, while pushing two fingers inside her pussy, and pumping her hard.

"Mine," I say thickly as I fuck her with my hand.

She's so wet that my knuckles make a squelching sound, and I can tell she's flushed all over, her neck, her face, as I sex her like I own her.

Her flushed body glistens in the candlelight, luring me to kiss every inch of it. I start with the cheeks of her ass, caressing and kissing them because I just worship this woman. I go up her back, tracing her spine with my tongue. And when she sighs and lifts her head, those red locks tumbling down her shoulders, the precarious thread of self-control that I still had snaps.

I release her wrists and fist my hand in her hair, hard. She makes a sweet little sound of pleasure instead of pain, and it's all I can do not to come undone before I even penetrate her. The pleasure is so harsh as I push myself inside of her that my balls tighten and my ass clenches so hard it hurts. I push through her tight walls that clamp on me hard.

"Fuck, you're so tight," I growl through my teeth, barely able to control the pleasure that builds up in my groin. I want to unfold myself inside of her. I even have this crazy vision of her with my cubs in her arms.

I knew from the first time that Melanthe Syke is a screamer when she comes, but when she comes for me now, her tight walls suctioning me inside her, I can't hold it anymore. I release my sperm, tugging her hair, my black and blue metallic fur beginning to sprout from my skin.

"You're mine, Melanthe." My voice is changing into the bestial voice of the wolf, fangs pushing out of my gums. "Mine to claim, mine to own, mine to love."

Her juice coats my cock, and the most beautiful sensation takes over me. I'm no longer sure where I end, and where she begins.

"The world might be against us." I say as we both descend from our high, easing myself out of her and turning her in my arms. "But I'll set it all on fire if it dares come between us."

The shifting process has stopped mid-way, and now it's started to revert, but my body is still hot, and I can use that for Melanthe's comfort. I lie down on the floor and pull her into my arms.

"God," she whispers, kissing my chest lovingly, her hands wandering over my torso like she's been dying to do this. "I never thought sex could feel like this."

"What we did wasn't sex, Melanthe." She looks up at me, and I meet those queenly bright green eyes. "It was love. Possessive, jealous, sick. But pure. The kind of love that only bonded mates can share."

"Now I feel bad for the rest of the world. Every single person out there should be allowed to experience this kind of love, at least for an hour in their lives." She smiles, and it feels like I'm seeing it for the first time. Her face is so youthful, I swear she's growing younger by the minute, and I have a terrible suspicion as to why that is happening.

But I don't want to worry her, not now.

I smile back and stroke her smooth cheek with fingers that still smell of her. She nestles close under my arm and licks my knuckles, then my fingers. My cock reacts. God, I could take this woman all night, every night, for the rest of my life, but even if we could spend our lives together, that would probably be too demanding for her.

Besides, forever is not in the cards for us.

"Melanthe, you and I, we share something special through this bond. It's unique, and unbreakable, but we can't live it out, not without destroying your life in every way possible."

"Achilles, nothing is worth having, if you're not in my life. And when you talk about destroying it, what exactly do you mean? That I'll lose my seat in the Council? I only wanted it in order to find out who it was inside the Council that helped the serpents. As for Charles' businesses, I wanted to make sure they stayed within Princess' grasp, that those sharks didn't jump to rip her off, but she doesn't actually need me to. She has Nero, and that ensures that she'll be happy forever, once she heals her wounds that Charles' murder left her with. As for me, I really don't want anything from Charles, I never have." She looks at the window as if gazing into her past.

I listen to her as she goes through her story with Princess' father, her arms wrapping tighter around me, and mine around her, until it feels like we're one body.

"As for the Reaper," she says in the end. "I think I know who he is."

Locking eyes, I know she has the same suspicion I do. I open my mouth to ask, but a boom rips through the hall, and through the magic we share. I jump up to my feet, hoisting Melanthe up too, and shielding her behind me to make sure no one can see her naked. The chapel doors have hit the walls, and people enter with lamps that resemble torches.

"What the fuck is this," I hiss. "A witch hunt?"

"Actually, it's an inspection," Sybil says with vitriol in her tone. She and her husband are leading the group, him in an open night robe, his hairy pink belly hanging over the waistband of his pants, while she's wearing the same transparent dress from before, the same denim jacket over it, the same sneakers. My brothers Nero and Hercules come around the group, their jaws dropping when they spot me.

I shield Melanthe behind me as she puts her robe back on, and I wish she'd stay there, but she joins me and hooks an arm around mine, defying the group.

"An inspection? Why?"

"We're in the middle of a war here," Nero says, his eyes darting from me to Melanthe, like we've done the most reckless thing ever. "People saw light and heard screams. They alerted us, of course. It could have been serpents."

"The people?" I repeat. "And who was close enough that they saw and heard there was someone in the chapel before you did?"

My eyes fall on Sybil. She plants her hands on her hips and pushes her chin out in what I know is vengeful defiance. She meant to expose us.

"It was me. I went to the kitchen to get something to drink, and the kitchen is close to the exit that leads here, to the chapel. I saw light, and when I got closer, I heard screams."

"Funny," Melanthe intervenes, measuring her from head to toe to make a point. "That you should dress up in the middle of the night just to go to the kitchen. Actually, I'm pretty sure you're wearing the same clothes you had on when I saw you during the day, hovering around Achilles."

Sybil stares daggers back at Melanthe.

"The only funny thing here is that you're screwing your bodyguard, Councilwoman Skye," she spews. "I must say you're good. I thought you were screwing the chauffeur. But it turns out he was only the gay cover for another affair."

Tanner comes in running, shoving people from his path. When he reaches the front of the group, he stares at Melanthe with the eyes of betrayal.

"I knew it," he says, pointing a finger at her. "You were only using me. All your sweet smiles, all those open doors you left with every rejection, you were just playing me. You were already fucking this guy."

"Oh, come on, Tanner, you're just mad that I used you before you got the chance to use me," Melanthe bites back, cocking an eyebrow at him. "You thought I was a needy widow that would fall prey to your charms in no time. You're right, I played you. Your attentions never impressed me. If anything, they offended me."

I know this whole situation has her mortified, but I think this woman could move mountains if she wanted to. She stands here proudly, as if the group pressure has nothing on her.

She has the entire group shifting their weight from one leg to the other, not knowing what to do with themselves. She has put them on the spot, instead of the other way around. The only composed people here are my brothers. Nero crosses his arms over his chest, glaring at me from under his eyebrows.

As for Hercules, he's busy staring at Sybil like she's the most despicable thing that ever existed, while her husband Clayton is so shocked he doesn't even look angry anymore. The angry V is gone from his forehead, his white hair frizzed. He looks utterly harmless, which makes one thing clear to me—he's not the one who supported the serpents from the Council. Fact is, neither is Tanner, as much as I wish it were him, so I can rip his head from his shoulders for only thinking about Melanthe that way.

"Wait a minute." Melanthe says, defying Tanner and Sybil, who are scowling like they could rip us apart if they had the power. She tilts her head to the side, expressing suspicion. "How do you know that my chauffeur is gay, Sybil?"

"It's common knowledge by now."

"No, actually, it's not."

"Not *all* your secrets are as safe as you think," she spews. "They all came to life one by one, just like your affair with Achilles finally did."

"Well, why don't we bring *your* affair with Achilles to light as well then?" Melanthe hits back, and the piglet gasps. He looks at his wife, and I can tell he wants to blurt out, 'How could you,' because the way Melanthe exposed the affair doesn't leave room for doubt, and maybe on some level he always knew. But the contempt in Sibyl's face is enough to stop him.

"Don't even," she says, looking at him like she could spit in his face. I always knew that Sybil was faking her sweetness, but I didn't think she was actually so poisonous. "What did you think, when I married you, that I did it for *love*?"

Her head snaps back to Melanthe, and this time, it's with the hatred that can only come from pure malice, or pure pain.

"Since we're at the moment of truth," she says, coming forward. I shield Melanthe with my arm, pushing her behind me, because a catfight becomes dangerously probable. Not that I don't believe Melanthe could take Sybil, but this isn't the time nor the place.

"Why don't you tell everyone here the whole truth, Melanthe. That you had been divorced from Charles Skye for four years when he died. You never really had a legal claim over his seat in the Council, or his legacy."

Complete silence settles over the chapel, and it's not only the silence of shock. The air thickens with the smell of threat. My eyes dart around the chapel. I can see my brothers feel it, too. They're standing still, focused, all their senses piqued. The only one who seems unbothered by this change in the air is Sybil.

"How do you know?" Melanthe demands, her chest pushing against my arm. There's no intimidating this woman, there's only angering her.

"You really can't see how? Sybil continues as if she wants to provoke some other memory in Melanthe. "Come on, I'm sure that if you try hard enough, you'll understand. No? Still need some help? Okay, I'll give you one word, just one. It will be enough to trigger the answer in your blood—sister."

As the word sinks in, Melanthe pushes my arm down, facing Sybil. She thirsts for more, but as she opens her mouth to speak, cool air blasts in, the shockwave sweeping people to the sides as if they were nothing but feathers, and making room for a tall man in a black suit that steps in through the doors.

He's got his hands behind his back, and there's something about him that speaks of death. Could be because he looks like a mortician, but then my brothers shift into their wolf versions twice their human size in a split second, growling so loud the chapel walls shudder.

There's no doubt left—this is the Reaper.

"Gentlemen, finally we meet," he says in a rasping, hissing voice. He's got a split tongue, that makes everyone's skin crawl. I can tell by the shudder that goes through them.

My brothers don't attack, they just watch him closely like beasts from the bushes. None of us expected this. This is bad news. Bad as fuck. We're not prepared for this.

"How did you get in here?" I grunt. His presence in our midst doesn't make any sense, the borders are sealed, the pipes, too.

"I live here, Mr. Wolf. I was here the whole time, since all of this started. Since your brother Drago took down Sullivan."

Sybil grins, and things start to connect in my head. It's only seconds until I see the whole picture, and that word, 'sister', suddenly makes all the sense in the world. Unfortunately, my seeing the whole picture comes five minutes too late.

"But how is this possible?" Clayton reacts, looking from Nero to Hercules, as if they were the ones responsible.

"It's possible, Mr. Ray, because the Wolves thought they were playing me. In truth, I was the one playing them," the Reaper says as he approaches, his slitted snake eyes fixed on mine. He's relishing this. "I have been playing them since the night I killed Charles Skye with my bare claws. They could have never guessed it was me, because I was supposed to have been trying to breach Darkwood Falls, and failed repeatedly. But you see, this palace has been in my family for many generations—long, serpent generations—and it has wings you never knew existed. Add that to the fact that us serpents like to dwell underground, and there you have it. The reason why no one. Ever. Knew." He rests a hand on his daughter's shoulder, Sybil's, his sharp serpent eyes darting over to his other daughter. Melanthe. *My* Melanthe.

She looks like the truth of this makes her sick to her stomach, even though both of us suspected it.

"I'm sorry we had to meet again this way, Melanthe," he says. "I planned to do things differently. Later. But then a Wolf brother imprinted on you, and things changed." He can't mask how much he resents that part. I grit my teeth, ready to shift and tear out his throat with my fangs before he can blink.

"Wait, what, you are Melanthe Skye's *father*?" Tanner cries in a girly pitch, staring terrified at the

Reaper like he were the plague. And in a way, he is. As a Grim Reaper, he is a bringer of death. Which explains Melanthe's youthful appearance—she has the supernatural blood of death itself flowing through her veins.

As if on cue, men with reptilian faces and black suits slither into the chapel. My brothers tense, their claws out, ready to take them on, but then more pour in.

"How did they get here?" I growl. "You couldn't possibly have had so many serpents on the inside. We would have caught their scent."

"Well, I let them in, of course," Sybil says with a triumphant grin. "Through the old aqueduct that supplied the well in front of the house until last week." She relishes the bristling anger in my face. "Don't you wish you'd treated me with more respect now, Achilles? You should have known better than to fall for someone else. For my uglier sister, no less." She speaks that word out with hatred.

"It's not something I can control, and you know it. Wolves don't choose who they imprint on."

"And it's not even of consequence, my dear," the Reaper says. "Because Mr. Wolf won't live long enough to enjoy either you or your sister. The reign of the Wolves ends tonight."

"That remains to be seen," Nero growls with death in is glowing eyes. Hercules prowls next to Nero, almost twice as large, his snout curling over deadly sharp teeth.

"Thank you, for putting yourselves right into my hands," the Reaper says, but his voice is no longer the same hissing rasp from before. It's tenser, and his snakes register that as their cue.

They shift in a snap, their heads morphing, their bodies shedding their clothes and their skin. They grab every single person present, including Clayton and Tanner, Tanner struggling and screaming like a girl. A dozen others storm in, surrounding the group and my brothers. Fuck, Sybil let in a whole army like a Trojan Horse. We don't stand a fucking chance.

The blood drains from my head, and the Reaper grins a grin that is too large, and oily, his teeth dark. Melanthe gasps, but she gets a grip fast, and looks around for something she can use to help. It seems she's looking for a weapon, my brave mate, but I won't let her even try to attack the Reaper. I'll die before I allow anything to happen to her.

"You and your brothers don't stand a chance, Mr. Wolf." The Reaper spreads out his arms, and laughs. "Finally I have the alpha trapped, and two of his brothers. Without the three of you, the others will be headless. Drago and Conan won't be able to defeat my armies alone."

"There are many wolves outside of Darkwood Falls," I hiss. "They will flood into the town, trap you all here, and massacre you."

"I'm not impressed by your threats, Mr. Wolf. As you can see, I had a reliable ally in my daughter here." He squeezes Sybil's shoulder, who keeps staring at me defiantly, searching for signs of despair in my eyes. But even if my heart does beat faster watching the people being held back with snake tails around their necks, and my brothers surrounded, my mind keeps searching for solutions.

"Leave Achilles and the others alone, Reaper," Nero calls in his growling alpha voice that makes the windows shake. "Fight me. I am the alpha of this pack. It's me you wanted this whole time."

But the Reaper doesn't turn to meet his eyes. He's taken a special interest in me. I imagine it might have to do with the fact that I fucked both his daughters, hurt one deeply, and fell in love with the other. He cannot tolerate any one of these things.

"I will take you up on that offer, alpha," he says, still fixing me with his reptile eyes. "But it's not you I'm going to fight one on one. I'll fight your brother. Achilles. Kill me, and all my serpents are to stand down, leave Darkwood Falls and never return."

"Great," I growl. "Let's begin." I flex my arms, fists balled and ready for battle, but Melanthe jumps in front of me.

"No! I love him. If you want to fight him, you're going to have to fight me as well."

"Later, sweetheart," he hisses, and a new wave of cold sends a shockwave through the chapel, practically blowing Melanthe away. I catch her before her body hits the wall, while the Reaper holds his other daughter in place. But only a second later, he unfurls from his own suit like a worm being born, shedding skin and slime. The mollusk-like body gets covered in scales within seconds, and he grows so fast and so big I need to step back. Fuck, he's even bigger than Hercules.

"Melanthe, Nero, Hercules, stay back," I call, shooting up to my full wolf size, my claws elongating, my fangs piercing through my gums, fluorescence blasting in my irises.

I howl, flexing my muscles, drawing energy from the night. But the large serpent doesn't waste any time. He moves as fast as a cobra, his body making a loud rustling sound against the chapel floor. He forces me backwards towards the altar, and I go along, thinking about everything we've learned about the Reaper's vulnerabilities along the years.

As a Grim Reaper, he is death in the flesh, and the cold breath of death has been in this chapel since the moment he stepped in. The only way to kill death, is from the inside. Inside his body. The plan had always been for my brothers and me to face him at least three at a time, and my brothers jerk forward to intervene now. But the other serpents tighten their tails around the hostages' necks, and they're forced to stand down.

Melanthe screams, and throws herself at the Reaper, but luckily Nero gets her and holds back in time.

"Now," the Reaper says, his reptile eyes swirling. "It's you and me, Achilles Wolf. If you manage to defeat me, the hostages will be free, and Darkwood Falls forever cleansed of serpents."

He snaps at me as swiftly as the wind, his fangs sinking into my shoulder. I growl, ducking under his large body and plunging forward. I slash at him in the process, cutting him with my claws, but even though he hisses in pain, the traces I leave behind close within seconds. I move out of the way quickly enough once, twice, three times, but he gets me again, and bites exactly into the same place he did before. White pain cuts through me, causing me to howl and Melanthe to scream, but now I understand his strategy. The bastard is gonna go for the same place until he tears me apart, or at least he's gonna try. I have to get something into that mouth of his the next time he tries. One of the torches, maybe, throw fire into his body, burn him from the inside out.

I manage to swipe one from one of the men, and stick it into his throat when he comes at me again. He chokes on the thing, making retching sounds, but his poison is spreading fast through my body. It's going to kill me fast, so I need to kill him faster. To finally rid the world of the great evil serpent Reaper, that will be my legacy.

But the torch breaks between his jaws, and he swirls around, hissing at me, his spit covering my face.

"Fuck," I growl. I need to find something else, and I need to find it now, no, I need to find it five fucking minutes ago.

Melanthe screams my name, her desperation ripping through my heart. I look at her, with all the love I feel, and the answer reveals itself to me, as clear as it is painful.

It slams through me like the poison the serpent Reaper has injected into my body, but I don't have the time to explore the idea or think of something else. The more I think, the more it will hurt anyway. So I decide to just do it.

I throw myself at him with all the strength I have left in my muscles, slashing at the uppermost part of his huge body, right under his chin. The flesh is still transparent and slimy there, not covered in scales, and it's the only spot that looks vulnerable.

He hisses and writhes as I run him by, slicing his throat in the process, his tail sweeping the benches and hurling them against the walls, where they shatter and fall in pieces to the ground. I draw him to the corner, and when he comes at me, his mouth open, his fangs glistening, his eyes swirling. I'm ready to do it.

I'm ready to throw myself into his huge mouth, crawl inside his body, and tear him apart from there.

But when he's just an inch away from my face, and my body tensed, ready to plunge into his like an arrow, he stops as if someone had thrown a lasso around his neck. He struggles against this invisible power, trying to come at me, but he can't. Only when he turns, looking behind himself, and clearing the field of vision for me as well, I see Melanthe.

She stands in the middle of the chapel, among the shattered pieces of the wooden benches, still as a statue. There's something of a warrior in her stance, her fingers curled like claws, her red hair tumbling down her shoulders, her white robe like the garment of a ghost. And she does spread the power of a ghost throughout the room, like invisible chains that make the other serpents writhe on the floor, the hostages free.

"Now," Nero calls, running over with Hercules, ready to help me tear the Reaper apart, but Melanthe stops them.

"No," she calls.

She fixes the huge serpent with her bright green eyes like a witch. "You won't be able to kill him anyway, even if you tear him apart. You'll only sacrifice yourselves for nothing. Trust me, I know. I tapped into the genes he left in my body. He can only be killed from the inside, but not just anything will do." She tilts her head to the side, addressing the serpent. "I don't know what your poison is, but I promise you, *father*. I will find out."

The serpent stares at her in disbelief, and she grins, this time with pleasure.

"I am your daughter. I have power over your serpents. And this was it for you." She glances over at Sybil, who seems frozen in place with an open mouth. "And for my sweet little sister. I know how to keep you hostage, and you are both going into the dungeon, until the Wolves figure out what to do with you."

"Actually," the serpent says, straining against her invisible chains. "Sybil is your older sister. But, like you, she doesn't age. I wish you girls a nice time as you get to know each other. And I wish you, Melanthe, nice mourning for the rest of your life. Because your bonded mate? He only has hours to live."

My brothers move closer, ready to grab him, but the Reaper uses the ace up his sleeve. The air turns ice cold, and the shockwave quickly follows. As weak as I am from the poison spreading through my body, it blasts me right through the altar doors. Just before I black out, I know—the Reaper escaped. And I'm going to die.

THREE DAYS LATER
Melanthe

THE PUREST JOY THAT ever existed fills my heart as Achilles finally opens his eyes.

"My love," I whisper, bending down to him and kissing his lips softly. "You're awake. The witch Cinzia's cure worked, you're back."

"What?" he rasps. His vocal cords haven't been used in days, and he squints at the light that filters through the curtains. "What happened?"

"You're safe. You're back at my manor. We all are."

"How?" He props himself on his fists and sits up, his tattooed body glistening in the firelight. He's a monument of power, even now, recovering from the Reaper's poison that almost killed him. "How did I survive?"

"Cinzia of the Witch Eyed Sisters made a cure, with the help of, well of." I really hate saying it, but it's the truth. "Sybil helped. The Reaper disappeared without her, so she was forced to help us. She made sure to state her terms for it, though."

"So she's in our power now."

"She is."

He looks around at my bedroom. I've been sleeping by his side all this time, waiting for him to recover from the poison, and I have no intention of leaving his side ever again. I almost lost him a few days ago. I'm sure as hell not going to waste another minute I could be spending with him.

"The Reaper has been banished, and the serpents that he left behind, well..." I still don't know how I feel about this, I killed them. I didn't calibrate my power right, since it was the first time I was using it.

Too little, and it wouldn't have worked. Too much, and it killed them all, and that hurts. Probably because on some level I'm one of them. They're my people. "They died. What I did, I think it was too much. It killed them."

He grimaces at the pain that seems to shoot through his body as he adjusts his position. "Melanthe, how— What happened back there? How did you do what you did?"

I shake my head. "All I know is that I was desperate to save you. I would have done anything. I was desperate for a tool, and then it hit me. I was the Reaper's daughter. I had to be able to use that to my advantage somehow. Whatever was in his blood, was also in mine. I think it was the desperation that helped me find the resources." I cup his strong jaw with both my hands, my eyes full of tears. "I couldn't bear the idea of losing you. Seeing him hurt you, right before my eyes. It triggered such pain and such rage."

"Melanthe, you shouldn't have put yourself in danger."

"If I hadn't done that, you would have sacrificed yourself. I could see it in your eyes, Achilles. You would have thrown yourself inside of him, and torn him apart from the inside out. That would have consumed you, and he might have been able to put himself back together after that anyway. I couldn't let you do that. Not without sharing your fate. I don't want to live without you, my life has no meaning without you in it."

Those yellow eyes fill with a passion that could burn down the town. It gives me the courage to go on.

"Achilles, I know it'll sound crazy to you, out of place and sure as hell our of context but I... I love you. I never imagined saying these words to anyone but Princess, but I love you more than I ever thought it was possible to love a man. I know this isn't right, our relationship. It's twisted, but after the fear of losing you... I don't care anymore, I don't care about what the Council, what the more powerful of the town's people will do against me. I just—"

"Melanthe," he says, his voice soft, but sovereign. "There is only one obstacle that would keep me from claiming you as mine, the way I crave to do it. Princess. How do you think she would feel if I were to, well, ask for your hand in marriage? And if you accepted? Because the rest of the world, after everything we've been through, they can go and fuck themselves. Let them just try and come between us, I'll tear them apart."

Yes, I want to be with this man, and I'll go against the entire world if I have to. I almost lost him in the nightmare that went down at the chapel, and I sure as hell am never going to risk losing him again. Nothing is worth the pain of being apart from him, and now that Princess had a change at heart, nothing can stand in our way.

"Princess was terrified of losing me during the entire time we were separated. Both her husband and I were trapped at Clayton's, while she was at Drago's place. Now that she knew Charles' death was something the Reaper had done with his own hands when Charles was no longer useful to him, things changed completely for her."

"Did you tell her about Charles?" he inquires carefully. "I mean, did you tell her what he did to you when you were little?"

I shake my head. "No."

"Will you?"

"No."

"Why? I mean, I know it's painful for you to talk about it, but you wouldn't need to go into the details. Just telling her why you needed to be away from him would completely reinstate you in her eyes, she would see, she would realize you were a saint to stay with him to the end, to give her a family."

"I can't take away from her everything she's lived with her father, Achilles. She loved him, and he adored her, and he was a huge positive part of her life. It would be cruel to take that away from her."

Achilles caresses my cheek with his fingers, intensity in his gaze. "I always thought that you were a remarkable woman. Now I know I you're a goddess. Under all that tough exterior there was always a selfless goddess with a beautiful soul. One that I'll never stop worshipping."

I smile, nestling my face in his huge warm palm. "Besides, it's not necessary to tell her about Charles. She and I are on the right track to build a healthy, beautiful relationship now. She was so tormented because of everything she'd said to me, and her accusations, that she gave us her blessing to have a whole generation of cubs, if that's what we want. So yes, Achilles Wolf. I will marry you."

Joy spreads over Achilles' beautiful face. He jumps from the bed, picking me up in his arms and swirling me through the air as if there's no trace left of the Reaper's poison in his veins. He spins me around, my body crushed against his rock hard chest. He stops to kiss me hard on the lips, holding me so tight that I get dizzy.

"I love you, Melanthe Syke," he says, his breath hot on my cheek. "And no one, and nothing will ever take you away from me. If anyone ever tries, it will be the last thing they do."

THE END

Looking forward to Melanthe and Achilles wedding? Stay tuned for the last book of this series in early 2021. To receive notification of the release, and of all Ana Calin's monthly releases join her newsletter here:

And scroll down for the other books in the series
Read all the other books in the series:

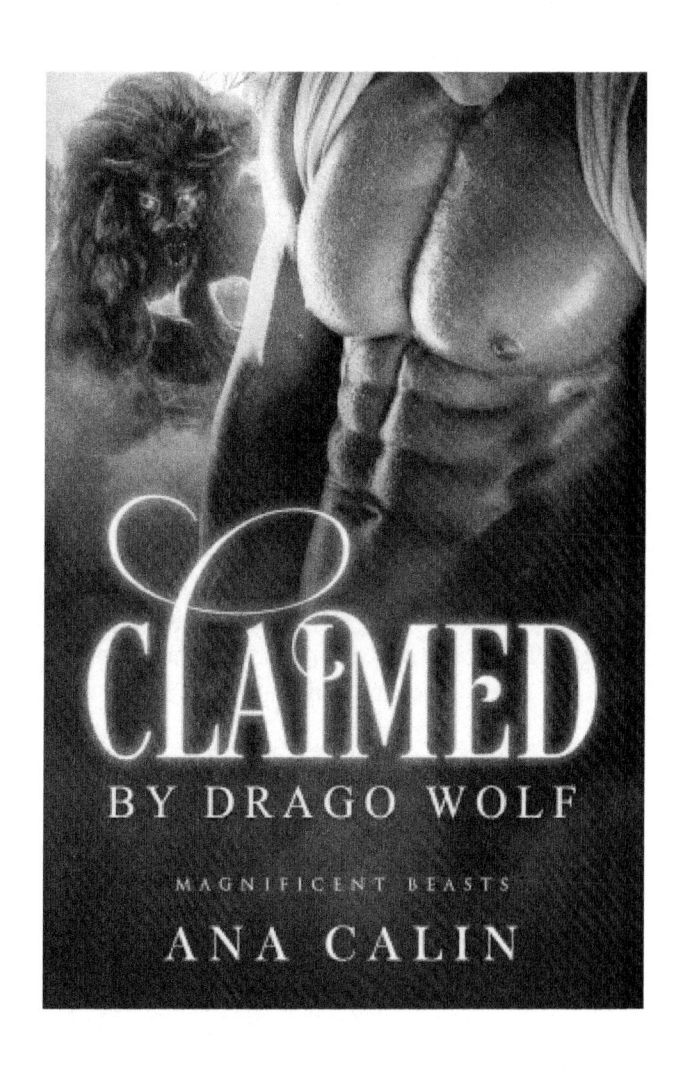

About the author

Ana Calin

Ana Calin writes dark and brooding vampires, brutally hot shifters, and fae princes with dirty secrets. Her books can be read as standalones, but it will enrich your reading experience to read them in order. Her most popular series is Fae of Darkness, closely followed by Fae of Fire and Ash, and Dracula's Bloodline. Aside from writing and reading, Ana Calin also loves to kick ass on behalf of freelancers, small companies and entrepreneurs against the "sharks" of bureaucracy in Germany.